Bells
on the
Bay
a birch harbor novel

ELIZABETH
BROMKE

BELLS ON THE BAY

Publishing in the Pines

White Mountains, Arizona

For Ed and Eddie

"Of the bells, bells, bells, bells,
Bells, bells, bells—
To the rhyming and the chiming of the bells!"
Edgar Allan Poe

PROLOGUE—NORA

1976

She sat on a particularly flat-topped rock in the craggy outcropping that stretched down to the water from the back of St. Patrick's parish.

To her left, Heirloom Cove and perfectly private, serene households. Old and quiet and minding their business.

To her right, Birch Bay—a secluded inlet that gave way to Lookout Point on its far end.

With her white dress tucked neatly beneath her legs, just the veil caught on the wind, dancing up and down against the chill, tickling her lace-sheathed shoulders.

The sensation sent goosebumps down her spine, and Nora's body shook. She ignored it, her gaze positioned firmly on Heirloom Island, that witchy old clump of land hanging by a thread out in the middle of the lake.

Not often did her time on the Island come into mind, even when it sat plainly in her view every single day. Those brief but everlasting years sequestered in lonesomeness among a would-be tight-knit bunch of misfits. Not all of them in *delicate condition*. But all of them outcast in some way, shape, or form.

When Nora was in a mood, a gray coat descended on her world. Anything beautiful was ugly. Anything peaceful was chaotic.

Even firmly in her twenties, she couldn't shake the mottled shades from her mind's eye. A young woman with everything ahead of her, Nora had just one hope at clarity.

Wendell.

Like a human lighthouse, he could guide her back to center.

Presently, however, he was yards away, inside the church, trying to smooth things over.

At the start of their ceremony, things were already smooth. As smooth as smooth could be for the lovebirds.

Nora's mother and sisters helped her dress in the religious education room, which was outfitted with a mirror and a smattering of plastic chairs for the bridal party. A bottle of aspirin and the water cooler were the only refreshments previous to the reception. Food would come after Mass. So would drink. Mrs. Hannigan was firm on this point.

Her father stood dutifully in the lobby, waiting for his second daughter—his middle child. Mr. Hannigan was always waiting for the Hannigan women. Much like Wendell. Much like any man in Nora's life, actually. Some lurked. Some waited. Her dad and Wendell weren't lurkers, to be sure. But there were one or two of those around. Impervious to social norms and Nora's reputation, no doubt.

Wedding guests peppered the pews, dressed a touch more warmly than they were used to for such events. The ladies wore light sweaters. Heavy shawls. Scarves throttled their necks, and thick pantyhose ran tenuously down into closed-toe shoes.

Wendell's family came, too. As a matter of honor, more

than anything. But still, their mere presence was enough of a boon to the attitudes of the day. It fortified Nora, and seeing them sitting there gave her a good feeling about the day.

Wendell's brother and a few errant aunts and uncles whispered mutedly as Nora's father walked her up the aisle.

Ave Maria played from a single organ in the loft, and a tear slipped from Nora's left eye and formed a rivulet through her makeup and down to her chin, clinging there until she arrived at the altar. Her attention was so fixed on Wendell that she didn't notice the wetness until he rubbed it off with his thumb and a sweet smile. Wendell did this first, before he shook her father's hand, and that maybe was in poor form.

Still they pressed on, clasping each other's hands as the priest began the Mass.

At the behest of Mrs. Hannigan, Father Bart offered a High Mass to celebrate the Sacrament of Marriage of their daughter to Wendell Acton.

Every so often, Nora tried to glance back at the modest crowd, assessing people's reactions to the whole thing. Hopeful that she and Wendell weren't alone in their glee.

Unfortunately, boredom shaded most of their faces.

But the boredom didn't last.

As the ninety-minute mark neared, even Nora felt light-headed and loopy. Communion bread wasn't enough to hold her over, and she soon understood why some brides fainted on their wedding days.

She didn't faint, though.

Not even when the priest directed the guests that if any of them had *a reason why these two should not be married, speak now or forever hold your peace,* and Wendell's mother shot up from behind them and answered, "I do."

CHAPTER 1—NORA

WENDELL ACTON CASE

I f I don't commit this to paper, then who will?

Clearly, the good Detective Clint Mathers has the answers he needs to sign the paperwork and sleep well at night. Unless, perhaps, he's playing the part of useless, small-town cop? Then again, maybe he really *is* a useless, small-town cop. Who's to say?

In the past year, the only information to surface in the case of my husband is the fact that there *is* no information.

If I were a betting woman, I'd wager a guess that someone in this town is withholding critical details. I just don't know who.

Funny enough, it's clear to me that Mathers and the rest are satisfied in the very lack of a firm resolution because they think they know what happened to Wendell. They think they know, and the town does, too.

You see, Mathers and the rest won't drag the lake or comb the woods because to them, there is no mystery.

Everyone in this forsaken *community*, if you can call it that, has established a theory and stuck to it. They haven't, however, lost interest. This much is true, and it's all that's keeping me hopeful. If they were utterly *disinterested*, then we'd really be in trouble.

Still, I am their maligned object.

When I go to Mass, I feel their stares.

At the market, they whisper.

And should the newspaper or the school or the charitable society turn up at my door one more time...

Maybe I'll just tell them what they *want* to hear. That *I* had something to do with Wendell's disappearance.

CHAPTER 2—CLARA

A brittle breeze whipped across the back deck of the Heirloom Inn, sending two paper napkins sailing into the air and across the grass.

"I'll get them," Clara declared, dashing down the steps and planting a foot on the first, grabbing it, and catching the second with her free hand.

She stood and shielded the sun from her eyes as a distant swell caught her attention.

Hooking her thumb behind her, she made her way back. "Have you ever seen a wave that high on a *lake*?"

"It's a gale," Kate replied, raising her voice and ducking her head to see the sky beyond the awning. "I'm sure we'll be stuck inside all weekend."

It was Thursday, and the Inn was dead for the night, so the oldest of the Hannigan sisters put on a simple happy hour. *Before winter strikes*, she'd said.

"Looks like this will be a short autumn," Megan commented, and Clara resumed her seat, pulling her sweater sleeves down over her hands and squeezing the spare fabric in her palms. It was perfect cuddling weather, and she'd rather be with Jake. Cuddling together to a cozy movie. That sort of thing proved rare for them. A teenage daughter, no matter how supportive, complicated matters, to be sure.

Amelia yawned and tucked her knees under her chin like a teenager. "We still have some good weather left. Next week, for example. It'll warm back up, you know."

"How's the theater stuff coming, Amelia?" Clara cradled her drink and took a slow sip.

Birch Harbor High was looking for an after-school drama club leader. After the last one retired, they decided to eliminate the course altogether and focus their fine arts funding on orchestra. When Clara saw the bulletin, she snapped a photo and sent it to Amelia, who called the school not five minutes later.

It worked out well because Sarah joined. Then Mercy and Vivi followed, and soon enough, theater was cool, and Amelia had something else to distract her.

She'd needed distractions, too, because she'd been behaving oddly ever since the lighthouse grand opening.

Not a single one of them could get her to open up, either. A quiet Amelia was a rarity and a sure sign that she may not be long for her current circumstances.

Each time Amelia was about to pack up and leave one town for the next—one role for the next, one theater for the next—she'd called her sisters, one by one. Clara had grown used to it: the one-sided phone call. Amelia beating around the bush, asking questions about *Clara's* life. About the weather. About anything that would tear the focus off her despite the fact *she* was the one to make the call. And then it would come out: *I have to get out of here.* Or *It wasn't a good fit.*

No real excuses. Just the announcement that a new

chapter was looming, and it was high time Amelia turned the page.

Perhaps that was the real reason Kate had called the happy hour. Maybe she also sensed the subtle boiling.

Amelia swallowed the last of her wine and glanced at Clara. "Actually, it's going well." A frown spilled across her mouth. "Really well."

Megan snorted. "Then why do you look so... disappointed? Is it the girls? Are they behaving?"

Shaking her head slowly, Amelia answered, "I'm not disappointed. I'm weirdly... *content*. Everything feels a little too perfect. We decided to do *Pride and Prejudice* and present it just before Christmas break. It's already cast. Sarah is Lizzie, of course. Mercy is Jane."

"Let me guess," Kate lifted a manicured eyebrow. Somehow, she was improving with age. Not in a way that Nora did —not with all the baubles and the false eyelashes and the nails—but with elegance. As though her efforts had been transferred almost entirely on herself. In many ways, Clara realized, Kate was on the opposite side of the spectrum from her. Whereas Clara was just starting a romance, Kate had been there. Done that. Now, settled and happy with Matt in what she was beginning to call their Common Law Union, she'd had her hair done, driven into the city for new outfits, and in a short span of time was twisting away from the trials and tribulations of a life lived on someone else's terms. She filled her own glass with whatever she wanted.

Could Clara do that, too? Live on her own terms *and* nurture a budding relationship?

"Vivi is Lydia?" Kate went on, dipping her chin.

Amelia held her hands up in surrender. "I didn't cast her. She *demanded* the role."

Kate and Megan laughed together, and the tension thawed.

"So," Clara broke in, "You get to direct *Pride and Prejudice* and suddenly life is perfect?"

Amelia blinked then frowned. "No. There's more to it."

Kate exchanged a glance with Clara, who had a follow-up question, naturally. "Such as?"

Clara stilled herself for an answer none of them wanted to hear. Something along the lines of *I found a great apartment in Chicago!* Or *There's a theater in DC that's just dying for a middle-aged spinster type. I know I can add ten years if I work at it!*

Instead, however, Amelia had a different revelation.

Something not a single one of them would have expected.

She pulled her handbag from beneath the table, and Clara caught a glimpse of the very corner of a black notebook. Her heart stopped.

It was a dead ringer for the one in the hope chest. The one labeled *Wendell Acton, 1992.*

Amelia pulled it out, slapped it on the table, and pulled something else out from her purse: a faded silver ring, delicate and ornate. Pinched in her fingers, it shone only just, and Amelia held up the notebook—not the infamous and secret one from the cottage. On its cover was a smear of silver duct tape that read: Hannigan-Matuszewski Wedding.

CHAPTER 3—MEGAN

Megan's mouth fell open.

"*Engaged*?" she cried out, looking frantically to Kate and then Clara, both more speechless than she, apparently. "To *Michael*?"

"Well, who else?" Amelia grinned mischievously.

"Hold on," Kate sliced her hand down on the table. "When did this happen?"

"At the grand opening. In the lighthouse." Amelia's eyes took on a misty effect. "It was... weird."

"Weird?" Clara echoed.

"Good weird," Amelia clarified. "It was perfect." Her brows knitted high on her forehead, and she shrugged. "Who would have guessed?"

"Oh my word, Am," Kate gushed. "This is *incredible*. We have a wedding to plan." Her eyes flew to Megan. "Is this up your alley, do you think?"

Megan considered it. She was in the business of setting people up, not marrying them. But could it be good for her brand? "Undoubtedly," she answered without hesitation. "We can put together a big advertising campaign featuring our first couple and how he proposed to her at one of our events. Blow it out. Really—"

"Exploit me?" Amelia dipped her chin and crossed her arms.

Megan cocked her head. "You love it, and you know it."

"I do not *love* it."

"You do love attention," Kate reasoned.

"What do you mean 'first couple?'" Clara interjected.

As she looked at Clara, she noticed a change. Something subtle. A small fierceness. A little fire in her. Megan narrowed her eyes on the youngest among them. "Oh, that's right. Technically, you and loverboy were my *first* couple." She pursed her lips but refrained from further teasing.

"Well, I don't know if we were the *first*, but you didn't set Michael and Amelia up."

"True," Megan allowed, "But they did—wait a minute. Are you saying?" Megan opened her eyes wider, glaring around the table playfully. "Are you and Jake *official*?"

Clara flushed pink, and a crack of thunder startled her. She jumped.

"You could have a double wedding!" Kate cheered. "Amelia and Clara marry Michael and Jake. How sweet would that be?"

"Let's make a triple. You and Matt. Right, Kate?" Megan pointed out.

But Kate shook her head. "No wedding for us. We're happy as we are. Settled. You can pretend we had a big blowout reception thirty years ago, if it helps you sleep at night."

"Okay, okay," Megan groaned. "Amelia, what do you say? Should we put the heat on Jake?" Out of the corner of her eye, Megan noticed Clara twist and fidget.

Amelia shook her head. "Plan their wedding, not mine. I think we'll keep it low key."

Megan pressed her finger on the table, pointing it toward the black notebook with scribbles on the front. "Low key? Looks like a wedding planner to me. Which, by the way, we can do better than that. You need a *white* binder with a transparent slot. Three rings. Pockets. Dividers. What is this, anyway?"

Amelia flipped it open, "Lists. That's all. We'll keep it intimate."

"I've got to be honest," Kate inserted, "Since when does Amelia Hannigan do anything intimately? You live your life out loud, woman."

"Not with stuff that matters. Not *this*." Amelia slipped the ring onto the proper finger and stared at it.

If Megan didn't know any better, she'd believe the rambunctious brunette. Maybe in all of Amelia's life, she hadn't been herself. Maybe she *had* been searching. And maybe now, she'd found what she wanted.

"Fair enough," Megan replied, meeting Kate's gaze and forming a silent understanding.

"Do we still get to plan a wedding, then?" Kate asked.

Amelia nodded slowly. "Yes. Definitely."

"At my field?" Megan asked.

"Actually, Michael says he wants to have a Catholic ceremony." Amelia kept her gaze down, and Megan could sense a bubbling turmoil. The seriousness and somberness of it all hit Amelia, who had no idea what to do with such a situation.

"A Catholic wedding?" she asked. "That sounds beautiful."

"Mom would be happy," Kate added, smiling and reaching for Amelia's hands.

Megan blinked. She, herself, hadn't had her wedding in the church. She and Brian consecrated their marriage later, after he convinced her that it was the right thing to do. The good thing.

It was, in the end.

"Let's talk about something else," Amelia announced. "We have plenty of time to discuss all that later."

"Plenty of time?" Kate asked.

"We have to take our marriage classes first, and I think it's a series of six or something."

"Six days? Six months?" Megan asked.

"Six weeks," Amelia answered.

She was serious about it. Megan beamed inwardly. But she knew better than to apply even more pressure on Amelia.

"Okay, well... Clara? How about you? Do you have any big news for us, then? Anything exciting?" Megan wiggled her eyebrows, deftly throwing the attention off Amelia (for once in their lives) and onto Clara (for once in their lives).

"Exciting? News?" A look of panic washed across Clara's face. "Like... what do you mean?"

"Whoa, whoa, whoa," Kate joked, sipping her drink and easing back into her chair. "I think Megan was talking about Jake. Remember? Your hot date around the lake? Oh, that rhymes. Jake. Lake."

"Oh, right," Clara's face cleared. "It was... amazing. We talked a little bit about life, and I think he likes me. Like, a *lot*."

"And do you like him... a lot?" Megan asked, knowing the answer but giving her kid sister a chance to talk it through.

"Yes," Clara replied. "I do."

Kate clapped her hands together. "In that case," she

declared, rubbing them swiftly together like she was about to play out a magic trick. "I nominate Jake and Clara to chaperone the girls' next sleepover, which is conveniently scheduled for Saturday night."

"Sleepover? Chaperone?" Megan asked. "Is Sarah involved with this one?"

Kate nodded. "Oh, yes. Sarah, Paige—who has elbowed her way back into the fold—and of course Vivi and Mercy."

Clara winced. "That's right. Um... we were going to..."

"Ohh," Megan chimed in. "That would be a good date night for you—to have Mercy out of the house." She looked at Kate. "You live here, can't you just let the girls have the attic again?"

"I can't," Kate answered. "I have a special guest."

CHAPTER 4—AMELIA

"Now who has a little intrigue?" Amelia winked at Megan then folded her hands on the table. "Spill, Katherine Hannigan. Who's the special guest?"

"Don't get too excited," Kate warned, staring at each sister in turn.

A memory tickled the back of Amelia's brain, and she snapped her fingers in revelation. "I know!" she cried, regaining some of her normal self after the third degree.

Being engaged was an oddity to Amelia. She'd wanted that for so long—she'd wanted someone to love her and commit to her forever and ever. She'd wanted it so badly that she'd almost given in to other, lesser specimens of the male persuasion. Now, here she was with Mr. Perfect and the reality of her antique heirloom ring and their marriage preparation classes with Father Vann—it was all too much. The woman who used to shine in the spotlight now felt like shrinking.

But it wasn't a bad thing. It was almost as though Amelia were shedding old skin and finding someone beneath who had longed to come out. A sensible, stable woman who Amelia had never known.

"Who?" Megan asked, bewilderment striking her features.

Amelia let out a sigh and settled comfortably into her chair. "Enemy Number One."

"Enemy number one?" Clara cocked her eyebrow.

Happy to fall back down the rabbit hole of all things Hannigan family history and drama (the kind that didn't directly involve Amelia, of course), she replied with a smirk. "Judith Carmichael."

Megan gasped. "That's right. You *mentioned* that before, but I was too preoccupied with the Sarah thing." The reference to events from the start of the school year felt age old, like it had happened in a different era. In a different world.

Amelia licked her lips. "Why on earth did you allow her to book a room? Do remind us."

Judith Carmichael was no friend of the family. She was the opposite, in fact. Someone who had tried to fundamentally thwart Megan's rising business. Someone to be wary of.

"She's not evil," Kate responded calmly, her hands pressed on the top of the table.

"Not evil?" Megan chewed on her thumbnail. "Don't turn that woman into some sympathetic character, Kate. You'll only set yourself up for trouble."

"And remember," Amelia added, her voice a warning, "She's married to Gene."

"But what's wrong with Gene?" Clara asked as innocent as a newborn. "He came clean, remember?"

"We don't know either one enough to form a judgment," Kate reasoned. "She's been by twice now and frankly, we've had good chats. And she... she sort of reminds me of *Nora*."

"*Nora*?" Amelia's eyebrows shot up her forehead.

"Yes," Kate replied earnestly.

"Then we *know* she's trouble," Megan added, reading Amelia's mind.

If Nora Hannigan weren't their own mother, the girls would assign her the same label: enemy. But she was their mother. And they loved her despite her hardness. Despite her cool effect. And besides, they were coming to learn quite clearly why their mother was the way she was.

Nora was no cartoon villain, twisting her mustache and snickering wickedly in the background. She was a fighter. She was a lover and a mother, *and* a sister. She was a good person who'd been through hell and back and didn't always strike the right tone. They all knew this about Nora, and they could joke about it.

But with Judith—what backstory could she possibly have to explain her bad behavior?

"I'm going to give her the benefit of the doubt," Kate said as she cleared the table. "Best case scenario, Judith wants to make amends and support a small business. Worst case scenario, I rented a room for a couple of nights and made some money."

"Really?" Amelia asked, suspicious. "I'd say the worst case is she tries to bring down the Heirloom Inn just like she did with Megan. What if they come here looking for intel? I just don't get it." Amelia shook her head and stood, slipping her notebook back in her bag and fingering Michael's mother's ring. It still felt that way to her—like it belonged to someone she didn't know. Some ancestor of another family. Not yet her own. *Yet*, she reminded herself.

"They?" Megan prodded. The four of them stepped into the kitchen one by one.

"Is Gene staying too?" Clara asked, wide eyed.

But Kate shook her head. "No. Just Judith."

"They need a break from each other," Amelia guessed.

Kate shrugged. "I have no idea. I mean—I'd imagine it gets old staying in that houseboat. They need something more permanent if they're going to spend so much time in Birch Harbor. You know?"

"Maybe they're on the market," Amelia suggested, thinking about the apartments and how she had a vacancy coming up in the spring. Megan, Brian, and Sarah would be out, in all likelihood, and Amelia would hate to lose rent.

"Maybe," Kate agreed. "But anyway, that's why the girls need a sleepover spot. I don't want any extra drama here. Hosting Judith will be more than I can handle." She gave Amelia a meaningful look. "The lighthouse? Maybe they could throw down some sleeping bags in the living room?"

Amelia shook her head. "Michael and I have our first marriage prep class at six, and I don't want them there without me. No offense."

Megan frowned. "After?"

"Dinner. To celebrate."

"Speaking of which, we need to plan an engagement party. *And* a shower. Oh, and then we have Thanksgiving and Christmas—" Kate was getting worked up. "So much to celebrate and so little time! You've got to give us your date. Soon, okay?"

Amelia smiled. "We'll talk about it Saturday. I promise."

Kate shifted the conversation back to the weekend. "Now, what about the girls? What's the plan? I won't be able to have them here whatsoever, and I know they plan to go out earlier in the day."

"Since when did teenagers have extravagant weekend plans?" Amelia asked, laughing to herself.

"Since these girls got together, that's when," Megan replied. "It's fine. They can make do at the apartment."

Kate lifted an eyebrow. "You sure? It's a little cramped in there—"

"The lighthouse isn't much bigger," Megan pointed out.

Amelia replied, "The lighthouse is twice the size of your apartment."

Clara nodded and lifted a finger. "They can have the cottage," she announced.

The other three turned their gazes on her, taken aback at the generous offer.

Kate shook her head. "No. You and Jake need your date night. You need space. Privacy."

"We're going to his place," she answered, biting her lower lip as if to brace for impact.

"Oh?" Amelia asked, her hand over her mouth. "Well, well, well..."

"It's just a movie. He's cooking. Maybe dessert... but they can have the cottage. No problem."

"I'll stay with them," Megan assured her.

Amelia looked back at Clara who surprised them again. "It's fine. Seriously. I trust them. Besides, what's the worst that could happen? They find another one of Nora's secrets?"

CHAPTER 5—NORA

WENDELL ACTON CASE

I'll start at the beginning, the day after he left, we suppose.

Friday, I set about investigating (I say *I* because it was just me at the start of this—as much as was possible with three teenagers and a baby. Mathers was more interested in tending to summer tourists than a local disappearance.)

Wendell hadn't called to say good night on Thursday, so I phoned the lighthouse until I spoke with his mother, who was surprised yet unmoved to learn there was something *off*. Her indifference was not, however, a surprise. Mind you, the Actons are the sorts who re-enter survival mode each morning they wake up, as though they're still crawling out of the Great Depression even decades later. They never shake that effect—the hungry, worn expressions of people who were in a losing competition against poverty. Unhappy.

That's what I think of them. A pair of unhappy folks who have grown too used to unhappiness. So used to it they aren't sure how to *not* be unhappy.

Wendell's mother was unconcerned, to say the least. Annoyed may be a more apt description. Still, she recounted the day before in clear, useless detail.

According to her: Wendell joined his parents for breakfast—grits—and acted normally. He left for town on an errand. He returned to the lighthouse to fix his boat engine (though his father emphasizes that it couldn't have been a major repair).

His mother left at about noon to shop for groceries. His father worked around the lighthouse and main house thereafter and heard Wendell come in at one point, make an extended phone call, and then leave again. No, his father didn't listen in on the call. In fact, he remained in the bathroom to offer his son privacy (this is exactly how the Actons are—they refuse to insert themselves in one another's business). His father left for the hardware store as soon as his mother returned—they argued in the kitchen over a second trip to town—gas isn't cheap! —and didn't happen to notice that Wendell had left.

I asked her if he'd taken his truck.

Well, she tells me, *yes, it's gone.*

That's when Wendell's father chimed in from the back. *Maybe he drove the boat to the house?*

I'd have rolled my eyes if it would do me good. Yes, this was a possibility. But *why?*

And then they remembered. *Never had the truck here!* his father hollered from the distance.

His truck was never here! his mother spat at me, despite the fact that it was *they* who were contradicting the facts.

And his boat? I pressed them hard, I did.

He'd been working on it, they told me. *It's not here, either.*

And later, when I spoke with the police, I found all of that to be confirmed.

Wendell's truck sat in the grassy embankment just beyond the shed, there at our house on the harbor. The keys tucked under the visor. The boat trailer sat empty in the boathouse. I could picture the scene as they described it to me. But that was all fine as long as he'd come back—as long as he was napping on the sofa or rummaging around in the basement, and his boat was in the water, tied off to our dock until he returned to the lighthouse to help his dad with this, that, or the other.

But he wasn't there.

And his boat was gone. Gone. Gone.

CHAPTER 6—KATE

Friday at precisely four on the nose, the doorbell chimed.

Kate was instructing Matt on hanging a family portrait in the parlor, and a quick peek out the front window confirmed that Judith Carmichael had arrived.

She paused, peering carefully from her secret spot behind the Chantilly curtain, and it wasn't until Matt joined her that she let the fabric fall closed again. "It's her."

He offered a curt nod and a tight smile. "It'll be fine."

"I know."

Shaking her hair off her shoulders, Kate smoothed her blue sweater and strode to the door, leaving Matt to wander off through the dining room and into the kitchen, where he'd disappeared onto the back deck. He'd mainly arrived for moral support, but his obvious presence might add to the awkwardness, rather than relieve it.

"Judith." Kate opened the door wide, stepping aside with it and bracing herself along the rough seam, her hand clenched around the knob. "Welcome back to the Inn."

Judith smiled and stepped in. She wore a button-down

flannel over a white, long-sleeved turtleneck. Cropped jeans spanned down her short, thin legs, stopping short of trendy brown booties. Her fingers wrapped around a leather bag—too big to be a handbag but big enough to contain what she'd packed for the weekend stay. Apparently.

"You've decorated for fall," Judith commented as her eyes darted past the oversized wreath on the door and into the foyer. Indeed, Kate had. When Judith had visited previously, she'd still had her late summer wreath up, along with a few Halloween-ish pieces and one or two autumn-themed items. But in the past week, she'd pulled out all the stops.

A trail of red and orange leaves curled across the front desk. Candles of varying heights gave off notes of cinnamon and apple. Pumpkins and squash nestled in hay filled the front hall table, where a sign read *Gather Here.*

The sign was meant to be inclusive, and she wasn't afraid to include Judith Carmichael, who by the looks of it had loosened up in the past week or two. "I just love fall," Kate replied. "The cooler weather, cozy fires—" She stopped short, catching herself gushing unnecessarily.

"Winter is my favorite," Judith revealed, stepping up to the desk and pulling a wallet from her leather bag. "My ID and card. Anything else?"

"Oh, thank you." Kate accepted both and set about registering her. "And no, that'll suffice."

Once she was squared away with payment, Kate rounded the desk and lifted her hand to the stairs. "I'll just show you to your room and let you get settled. Light snacks are available in the living room behind you." She gestured with the other hand back through to the living room then pointed back the other way. "We serve sherry at eight o'clock in the parlor."

"Sherry?" Judith arched an eyebrow. "My, what an old-fashioned sort of nightcap."

"My mother drank it." As she said it, Kate couldn't suppress a small smile as she turned and began up the staircase. "Funny, maybe."

"Oh, no. I think it's quite charming. That's just like Nora, you know."

Kate stopped, and her cheery expression fell away. She twisted to Judith. "Amelia mentioned you went to school together. Did you know each other beyond that?"

"No," Judith answered icily. "Not really, no. We both... changed. She especially, but even I outgrew those girlish years. She probably didn't even recognize me the first time we saw each other some years later."

"Oh?" Kate asked, her jaw tensing as she put one foot in front of the next, climbing carefully up to the second floor. "I didn't know you were so closely acquainted."

They arrived at the first room on the right in time for Judith to reply "Like I said. We weren't. Ships in the night have exchanged more words than Nora and I ever did."

"Right." Kate pressed her lips in a line, then pushed the key into the doorknob, turned it, and opened the door. "Well, here you are. Like I said. Snacks downstairs. Sherry at eight. I suppose you can find your way to a restaurant should you want more than that."

Without waiting for a response, she left the key in the knob and swiveled away, desperate to find Matt. Desperate to extract herself from the woman. Desperate, too, to extract herself from some *stranger's* memory of her own mother.

CHAPTER 7—CLARA

"You're sure the girls can have the cottage?" Jake asked when he arrived to collect Clara and drop Mercy off on Saturday night. Worry filled his eyes, but she brushed him off.

"Of course, I'm sure. Sarah is almost eighteen, and Megan and Brian aren't far."

He looked past her as Mercy joined Sarah and Paige on the sofa, where the older two had set up camp.

Clara could sense his fears. That they had a recent history of conflict. That it was awkward to exchange one girl for another—or one girl for one woman, rather. He was out of his element.

So was Clara, though. And two anxious people didn't necessarily cancel each other out. She glanced once more over her shoulder, her eye landing on the kitchen table, which she'd filled with special snacks and sleepover treats.

Clara didn't get to enjoy many sleepovers. The first one she ever went to, when she was in the sixth grade, turned her off to the whole thing.

Her mother had sent her to it with a solar sleeping bag

—something that she'd found at the church's annual swap meet, no doubt. Clara was already a misfit among the group of girls—forced into their posse by a well-meaning mother. Once lights went out, and the giggles subsided, Clara twisted to reposition herself in the confines of the bizarre sleeping bag. Her heal rubbed a low squeak against the aluminized film, and the rest was history. Clara was immediately accused of having bodily functions—something no girl should have at the tender age of twelve.

She never attended another sleepover again.

Therefore, it was important she set things up just so—that way no guest at Sarah's little get together would go to sleep a victim.

Five neatly folded blankets—and every pillow Clara could scrounge up—lined the fireplace hearth.

Apple cider and hot cocoa sat ready for preparation on the bar.

The kitchen table was stocked with cookies and sweets, popcorn and a savory platter of cut veggies. No soda or fruit.

Then, to kill two birds with one stone, Clara planted a heap of distractions.

On the coffee table, she carefully laid out a myriad of teen magazines—the good kind—and stacked a generous tower of DVDs (Clara didn't subscribe to much in the way of cable or streaming platforms, so DVDs were it). Rom-coms and even a couple of scary movies laid in wait.

But that wasn't all.

Then there was *it*.

The one thing Clara *needed* someone else to deal with sat there too, hidden among her own nondescript stack of reading material—a few literary journals, TIME, and some old paperbacks: Nora's black notebook.

The one that Clara couldn't face.

The one that needed to be found.

Was it a risk to plant such an important document in the hands of teenagers?

Sure.

Was Clara a risk taker?

No.

But she had also made a commitment to leave the past in the past.

She turned her phone all the way off, stowed it in her purse, and slipped her hand into her boyfriend's.

"Let's go." Clara squeezed Jake's hand, pulling him away from the house. Away from the drama. And into the future.

HE DROVE her down to Harbor Ave then cut west, up Cherry Hill.

"Wait a minute." She leaned forward and frowned. "Do you *live* in Harbor Heights?"

Chuckling, Jake shook his head and turned up a dirt road that veered north of the community. "Nope. We've got our place up this way." He jutted his chin forward, and Clara followed the gesture. She'd never been in the backwoods of Birch Harbor—if you could call them that.

Red and yellow-leafed trees lined the road, which grew narrower the further they drove. Her stomach twisted, and she swallowed. "I didn't know there were houses out here."

"There aren't," Jake replied, throwing her a side grin.

Frowning, she leaned back. "There aren't?"

Again, he laughed—this time more nervously. "Sorry. I promise I'm not driving you out to the woods." He glanced her way, then went on, "We have a cabin. It's small—just two bedrooms. Belonged to Mercy's grandparents. They used it for hunting. As a retreat and all."

Clara's body relaxed, and she let out a breath she didn't know she had been holding. "Oh." Blinking, she asked, "Mercy's grandparents are from the area?"

"Yes. Partly why we came here. Close to the water. We had a place. Worked out well. And Mercy gets to be near her ancestors. Or the memory of them, at least."

"What was their name?"

"Oh, um. Let's see... well, it's her maternal grandfather's side. So, Mathers. The Mathers. I think he was a cop or something like that."

Clara nodded, but the name sounded only vaguely familiar. Sometimes, even in small towns, one couldn't possibly know everyone. Not even when everyone knew *you*.

The truck slowed as a second dirt road appeared to the right, Jake and Mercy's daily passing having worn both equally.

Over a hundred yards off, she could spy a small cabin— exactly how one might picture a little leftover thing from generations past—used mainly for hunting, perhaps. Fishing, too. Out of place in the harbor town but appropriate there—buried among fir trees and pines.

Clara dared to roll her window down, the bitter chill of fall descending through the heavy topiary and settling at her shoulder as she reached a hand outside. "It feels different out here."

He looked over at her. "Different?"

"Dry. Woodsy." She took a breath of the air. "Manly." A giggle escaped her lips.

Jake gave her a side glance. "Manly?"

"I don't know. Yeah." It occurred to Clara that she hadn't

spent a whole lot of time in the company of a man. Alone, particularly.

"Just wait," he replied, "Mercy's the one who fixed up the inside."

After parking, Jake jogged around and opened Clara's door before she'd even scooped her purse from the space between her feet.

He led her up three quick steps and onto a tidy front deck. A creaky-looking wooden chair stood beside the front door, which was hidden behind an aluminum screen door.

Jake opened the screen, slid his key into the second door, and pushed it open.

The smell of fresh-cut pinewood hit her first, then her eyes adjusted to the dimly lit space. The kitchen shared long, knotty wood flooring with the living room, but the two were immediately distinguishable thanks to carefully organized furniture. An overstuffed leather loveseat divided the two areas, and a braided rug drew circles between the sofa and a modest entertainment center. Behind the sofa back was a narrow black floor runner that directed traffic back toward three doors. On the right of the runner, a potbelly stove ran from the floor through the roof, effectively segueing into the kitchen. There, a round oak kitchen table with four knobby chairs gave way to more old-timey effects, including an old white fridge and cookware that looked more appropriate for camping than for dining.

On the table, two perfect settings laid in wait, and a single candle leaned crookedly—only just—toward the window, as if searching for a light of its own.

Squat checkered curtains sat on either side of dainty lace ones, and that's when Clara noticed Mercy's hand.

Little feminine effects glowed from nooks and crannies. Glass picture frames and silver vases—each fitting less than the one before. A true hodgepodge and yet, it all worked together.

"It's not much," Jake said, letting out a brief cough and tucking his hands into his pockets.

"It's perfect," Clara breathed. "Like a little hidden gem. I doubt anyone in Birch Harbor knows about this place."

"They do, I'm sure. I mean, older folks do, at least. When we left the city, we sold most of our things. I couldn't much stand to see the same stuff I saw when Mercy's mom—"

"I understand," Clara whispered. "Surely, though, you kept *some* things?" She bit her lip, willing away the judgment in her voice. "I'm sorry; I didn't mean anything."

"Of course we did." Jake stretched a finger to the lace curtains and the candleholder. A bookshelf in the corner. "She's everywhere."

Clara swallowed. "Right. That's... *good*."

"We're moving on, though," Jake continued, clearing his throat and pulling a chair out from the table. "We're doing okay, is what I mean." He gestured. "Here, please take a seat."

Dinner carried on sweetly if awkwardly. Jake overcooked the salmon, but that was fine by Clara. They chatted about lighter affairs. Her school days. His hours at the marina. Mercy was noticeably absent from the conversation, but not in an uncomfortable way. Simply an intentional way. As though Jake truly meant to reserve the evening just for them.

She wanted to ask about his plans for building a place on the Island, but dinner had finished, and something hung in the air between them. A segue of some sort.

"Dessert?" Jake asked, clearing their plates.

"Of course," Clara replied, rising. "But please, let me help."

"All right, then," he allowed, and she followed him the short distance to the fridge, where he withdrew carrot cake. "This will be the best part of the meal, I assure you."

"It looks amazing," Clara agreed. "Did you make this?"

She spotted a serving knife on the counter and wielded it cautiously.

"No. Mercy did." He chuckled beneath his breath. "It was her... *test*."

"Test?" Clara lifted an eyebrow, and they carried their plates back to the table.

"If you don't like carrot cake, she won't trust you."

"Ah," Clara grinned, "right. Well, it seems to me that we've already established something of a foundation. Will it all come crashing down if I pick at this?" She gestured with her fork to the moist slice, raisins popping out here and there.

"I won't tell if you do." Jake's voice dropped, then his gaze did too.

Clara grinned to herself and dove into the cake with the full vigor of a woman starving.

And, in many ways, that was exactly what she was.

CHAPTER 8—NORA

WENDELL ACTON CASE

I must have called Wendell's parents back a billion times in the next twenty-four hours. His mother acted that way, at least. That my worry was a burden. My fear a nuisance.

And still, when I pressed them—both his mother and his father—on why they weren't concerned or suspicious, they reported that *surely, he must have left to go back to the house on the harbor* at some point.

Wendell's father ruminated on the probability that Wendell had had a falling out with me over the phone.

But then, I reminded them, why would he take his boat and leave the truck? Where could he have gone on the water and not returned? The police had claimed to have searched Heirloom to no avail. No other nearby community ever reported sight of him. Why wouldn't he tell *someone* if he was fed up with his marriage and running away?

More probably, I pointed out, he had left on a different errand altogether. North or south to get a part at a different marina, maybe. Or what if it was just a day on the lake? What if something *happened*?

I asked again about the boat repair and was met with a second, different answer. His father said then that the boat was in fine shape. It needed no repair whatsoever!

So, then what was Wendell doing with it?

Fiddling, his father had answered.

This didn't sit well with me, and I pointed out the discrepancy. That just the morning prior, the boat needed a minor repair. Mr. Acton was either lying or suffering from significant memory loss, I accused.

I may have been stressed during this particular conversation. The worst in me may have come out. I had a newborn, and I had the girls, and I had a cross-country journey to make. One I regretted making in the first place. Why couldn't I have been stronger for Kate? For the others? For Wendell and for myself? Why did I have to hide?

During that phone call, Wendell's mother came on and demanded to know why in the world I had left him for an entire summer. Where had I gone, and what was I doing there? And in the heat of the moment, I retreated to the company line.

A private family matter.

This was the wrong thing to say, of course. Especially to a *member* of our family.

And that's when the Actons hung up the phone and never answered it again. Nor did they call.

I suppose in their mind, I had dismissed them so utterly that I deserved to be left. Maybe they even hoped that that's exactly what Wendell had done.

Then again, those Actons were still in their survival mode, and I seriously doubted that his absence was much more than a blip on their radar.

The thing of it was, this would be the final strike between them and me. Already, they considered Wendell's marrying a Hannigan a grave betrayal. The earliest Actons weren't mixed up with the settlement wars of the early 1900s. They kept distinctly out of it—as was their mild English nature. The Hannigans, nearly brutal over the whole thing, surely set a bad name for themselves, and Wendell's parents clung to that reputation and applied it to me well past our first date.

Well past our wedding.

And they probably will until the day I die.

And if—*if* they do know anything about Wendell's whereabouts, they'll be sure to keep it from me. Of that, I'm certain.

CHAPTER 9—SARAH

"Truth or *dare*." Vivi's eyes glowed as she snarled the threat above the coffee table to Mercy.

Sarah and Paige were two years too old for games like truth or dare. Unless there were boys around, but Sarah wasn't about to invite any. Still, she stretched into a yawn as Mercy squeaked out yet another *Truth*.

"Have you ever kissed anyone?" Vivi asked, cloying. It was clear to Sarah that Vivi already knew the answer. They were best friends, after all. At least, as of the summer they were.

Mercy stole a meek glance at Sarah who offered a soft smile. "It's okay. I didn't kiss anyone until sophomore year."

Squeezing her eyes shut, Mercy whispered something low.

"What?" Paige asked, tossing a handful of popcorn into her mouth.

Vivi gave the two older girls a knowing look.

Sarah's eyes grew wide. "No way!" she cried. "Who? When? Does your... does your *dad* know?" A delicious smile curled over her mouth, and she sat upright on the sofa. The game was turning interesting, after all.

"Homecoming. After, before we left. Between the gym and the library, and it was *super* weird." Mercy pulled her pillow up to her face and mumbled something else.

"What?" Vivi tore it away.

"Does that make me a bad person?" Mercy repeated, wincing hard.

Sarah rolled her eyes. "It makes you normal."

"Too bad we can't invite boys here now," Vivi pouted, crossing her arms over her chest.

"Who wants boys at a sleepover, anyway?" Sarah answered. "This is a girls' night."

"Boys always make sleepovers more fun," Paige shot back, wriggling her feet behind Sarah's back.

"Get real." She grabbed a handful of popcorn, too, then slid a magazine from the coffee table. "Let's change games."

Vivi held up a hand. "No, wait. I want to hear about this *kiss.*"

Mercy pleaded silently to her friend.

"She doesn't have to kiss and tell," Sarah reasoned. "Right, Vivi?"

It was easy to rein Vivi back in lately, and Sarah didn't *un*enjoy her newfound power there.

"If she isn't technically kissing and telling, then did she even complete her turn?" Paige asked.

Sarah gave her a look. "Yeah. She told the truth. This isn't an interrogation. It's a dumb game." She pointed to the table of contents in *Teen Femme*. "Look, they have a M.A.S.H. game in here."

"Come on, Sarah. I haven't had a turn yet," Vivi whined.

"Fine, whatever." Sarah read an article about Women in Leadership as Paige shifted again.

"Okay, Vivi. Truth or dare."

"Dare, of course," Vivi answered coolly.

"Dare. Okay. I *dare* you to invite Mercy's little boyfriend here."

Vivi shook her head as Sarah dropped the magazine on the sofa. "Let's watch a movie."

Paige stood from the sofa and reached across the coffee table. "I'll do it for you then." She snatched the phone that sat idle in front of Mercy and scrolled.

"No, Paige, knock it *off*." Sarah tried grabbing for it. As she did, she tripped forward, landing with the heels of her hands into the pile of books and DVDs at the far side of the table.

The stacks slid off and onto the thick rug, landing with little fanfare.

"Fine." Paige passed the phone to Sarah as she regained her balance.

Mercy took her phone back from Sarah, acting wounded and even more nervous than before, and Vivi set about picking up the mess.

"Like I said. I think it's movie time." Sarah grabbed from the pile as Vivi restacked.

"Aw, I never saw this one." Paige plucked the one Sarah had grabbed. "*Little Women*."

"What about *Pride and Prejudice*?" Sarah wiggled it.

Mercy made a face. "I've seen it a million times, personally."

Vivi had finished stacking the DVDs and busied herself with the books and magazines, absorbed, apparently. Paige withdrew another one. "*What Lies Beneath*?"

"Too scary," Mercy complained again. This time, she grabbed from the stack. "Here. This could be good. *Flubber*. It has Robin Williams."

Sarah exchanged a look with Paige before cocking her head meaningfully at the younger one. "You're joking." Then she shook her head. Not at Mercy, but at the movie and at Clara, rather. Of course, it came as no surprise that her aunt's oddball tastes seeped into all aspects of her life. To be fair, *Flubber* wasn't oddball (Sarah had loved it as a girl), but it was oddball of Clara to leave it as an option for them.

"Oh, look. This is *perfect*." Paige thrust a DVD at Sarah.

"*Bride Wars*?"

"Yeah. It's funny and girly and perfect for a sleepover. Especially if we don't have any *boys* to cuddle up with."

"Fine by me," Mercy agreed.

Sarah grabbed the box from Paige and started around the coffee table. "Vivi, sound good to you?"

She made it to the TV, but Vivi hadn't replied.

Sarah glanced down to see the white-blonde hair shake enthusiastically just as she pulled her blanket over her lap, slipped one final book onto the previously toppled stack, and tipped her head up. A thousand-watt smile glowed from her face. "What? Oh, the movie. Yeah. I like scary stuff."

CHAPTER 10—MEGAN

Come Sunday morning, after she finished her shower and set the coffee, Megan unlocked her phone screen to find a text from Sarah.

Went great! We're going to the Inn to see if Aunt Kate will let us take the boat out.

Relieved to hear it went well, she settled into the sofa and flipped on the TV, surfing for a good guilty pleasure show. As she did this, she tapped Sarah's name to put a call through.

"Hey," she said, after Sarah's groggy morning voice came on. "Before you go to Kate's, you'd better give her a call. She has an important guest this weekend, and I'm not sure she wants to be interrupted."

"Can you call for us, Mom?" Sarah begged, coming to life. "Please?"

Megan hit speaker and swiped to her weather app. "Hang on a sec," she answered, reading the forecast. "It's nearly freezing out. Are you sure you want to go on the water?"

Sarah said something off the phone to one of the other

girls before coming back on, her voice lower now. "Mercy wants to meet her boyfriend at the dock, but she doesn't want to look *obvious*."

Megan let out a short laugh. "Then just walk around the marina. Grab a soda from the deli or something," she replied.

"That's not close enough. He works on the dock, Mom. He'll never notice her if we don't have a reason to be *on* the dock."

"Well, what about Mercy's dad? Why doesn't she just go visit him in the office there? Or take one of his boats?"

"Mom," Sarah whined. "The whole reason we're going this morning is because Mr. Hennings is *not* there right now. He has the day off. Mercy needs to capitalize."

"Oh, right. Right." Megan suppressed a smile. Still, she knew better than to cause a problem for Kate... or herself or any of the girls. Judith Carmichael wasn't to be taken lightly. "Okay, well, what about Vivi's dad? Maybe he can let you take his?"

Still unused to lake culture, Megan and Brian had become largely lax about Sarah cruising the lake in a boat, as long as she was following the rules of the water: chaperone and life vest.

But this also meant that Megan forgot that Sarah was the lone teen in her social group with such privileges.

"Matt doesn't let Vivi take the boat. Like, *ever*. Remember?"

"Mm, I forgot." Megan poured herself a mug of coffee. "Isn't there something else you can do to gain a little attention? Maybe just walk the beach?"

"I'll call Aunt Kate," Sarah huffed, and Megan grinned again. If there was one way to engender independence in a young person, it was to be totally and utterly useless to them. An odd parenting strategy, but it proved itself out as Sarah became more and more comfortable in her own skin, settling well into the culture of Birch Harbor.

"Before you go," Megan stopped her.

"Yeah?"

"Be sure to text me and let me know once you're out there, okay?"

"Yes, *Mother*."

"And Sarah," Megan added, "get permission from the other parents. Don't sneak out there and cause more drama."

"I know, *Mom*."

"Oh, one more thing, Honey," Megan knew she was pushing her luck.

"Ugh, Mom. Seriously."

"Who's your chaperone?"

"What?"

Megan sighed. "Who's driving the boat?"

"Paige's older sister can meet us and drive."

"Not Clara?" Recently, Clara had become the designated teen chaperone—she didn't seem to mind getting to know the girls outside of school, and Amelia had been too distracted.

"Um, we didn't ask Clara. We've got Paige's sister."

"Okay, well, put Clara on. I want to make sure everything went well."

"Mom, just call her phone. Come on."

"It'll take two seconds; just pass her the phone."

"I can't. She's not here. Gotta go, Mom. Bye."

CHAPTER 11—AMELIA

Sunday morning, Amelia awoke chilled to the bone. She generally preferred to keep her little house cool —opting in favor of the old potbelly stove rather than the furnace. But the temperatures had dropped too steeply the night before. She tossed and turned, too frigid to crawl from her bed and find a thick pair of socks or a second blanket. But too cold to sleep, either.

Finally, at half past seven, she forced herself up and grabbed a flannel robe from the back of her bathroom door.

She'd not yet unpacked all of her winter wear from their bins—it wasn't *quite* winter, after all—but her fuzzy slippers had happened to sneak into her closet anyway, and she stepped into them before making her way to the kitchen and fumbling with the thermostat until the heater kicked on.

She set about starting her coffeemaker, then swooped back into her bedroom where she recovered her engagement ring from the vanity.

Michael was due for breakfast—their Sunday ritual. This weekend, she was set to host, and pancakes were on the menu.

The ring was a touch too small for Amelia's finger, but not too small to fit. Just too small to make it easy for her to take on and off. Then again, she wasn't sure if perhaps she ought to just keep it on at all hours of the day and night. It was a silly question to ask her sisters, and if she asked Michael, she feared she might somehow reveal herself as a crock. A fake. The sort of woman who didn't know such simple womanly things.

Every night and morning since Michael's proposal, she dutifully tugged it off and wiggled it back on.

The evening prior, after their first class with Father Vann, Amelia and Michael had talked seriously about wedding plans, arriving on some decisions without much disagreement.

So far, they'd settled on a *mature* affair, as Michael called it. Amelia liked that. She felt that this wedding wasn't meant to be some flashy musical but instead, something sensitive and serious. The truest thing she'd experienced in her life to date. No acting. Just bliss.

No bridal party save for the witnesses. For Michael, a veritable loner, that would be his closest male relative—a much younger cousin by the name of Danny. Amelia hadn't yet met Danny, who lived in Detroit but planned to come for Christmas.

Amelia had no clue which of her sisters was the best fit for the title. Kate was reliable, yes. And they had been close as young girls. But in high school, Megan and Amelia were inseparable. Then again, it's not like the witness was a maid of honor. Or matron. And there *were* no bridesmaids. Or matrons. Amelia just needed one single woman to be her witness.

During their class with Father Vann, she had learned that the witness would also be her sponsor for the class and stand up for her during the ceremony. Such a person had to be confirmed by the church, married, and their marriage must have been consecrated.

Only Megan fit this bill, and that was a problem. If Amelia chose Megan, then Kate and Clara were left out.

She pushed the thought away and whipped together batter as a pat of butter sizzled to life on the skillet.

"Knock, knock!" Michael's voice came from outside the door.

Amelia set her batter down and strode to the door, unlatching it and swinging it wide open. "My Michael," she cooed.

He stood on the porch with a small, fresh bouquet of flowers sprouting from his grip, a broad smile on his face. "My Amelia."

Her stomach churned with excitement, and she stepped into him, slipping her hand into his free one and pushing up to kiss him on the cheek. "I just started breakfast. Come in."

He stomped his feet on the mat, then crossed the threshold as Amelia whisked the flowers off to an oversized mason jar. "Think these'll fit?" she asked as she ran water into the glass.

"What's this?" Michael asked behind her.

Amelia turned on one heel, the flowers leaning whimsically this way and that. "What?"

He pointed to the notebook page she'd left open.

Generally speaking, Amelia was no planner. But her own wedding presented an opportunity. Not to change her rotten ways or to be somebody she wasn't. But to see something through for once.

"Oh, right. My sponsor." She pressed her palm against her cheek. "Michael, I don't know. I don't think Kate could count since she's widowed—but maybe I'm wrong there. And if I chose Megan, then Clara is left out anyway. Maybe we *should* have a bridal party? To be fair?"

He shrugged. "Whatever you want. I'm onboard for whatever."

She nodded and poured a shallow pool of batter into the skillet. "I think intimate is best. And the whole idea is to have someone to give you marital advice, right? Maybe there's a different way to include Clara and Kate?"

"I'll tell you one thing, I picked Danny for three reasons. One, he's got a solid marriage. Two, he's family. And three, he's Catholic."

Amelia frowned. "I think I'll have all three of my sisters stand with me. You know? How can I not?" She set the spatula down on her dishtowel and crossed to the table, spinning the book toward her and making a note of her decision. "Megan can be my religious sponsor. All three can stand up with me at the altar."

"I think that's a good plan," Michael agreed. "Hey, let me help with that." He stood and followed her back to the stove where they danced around each other, finishing the pancakes, pouring coffee, and acting generally like a couple who had the same rhythms. The same patterns. *Chemistry*, even.

There was only one thing missing lately, and that was any attention to Wendell's case. Amelia was between a rock and a hard place, though. To bring it up meant that maybe she'd lose Michael to that all over again. But not bringing it up killed her. Could she bear to stay in town—get married in the same church where her parents were married—without answers?

She thought not.

"Okay, so—family only at the ceremony. Reception at the country club?" Michael asked as they sat together to eat.

"I think Megan hoped to host a reception at the house on the harbor, actually. Or maybe even the lighthouse," Amelia replied between bites. Amelia didn't particularly *want* to celebrate her wedding in her own backyard. Or her family's backyard.

She wasn't sure she wanted much of a celebration at all, in fact.

But that didn't mean she didn't want to be married to Michael. To feel safe in their union. To know that he was sticking around for good. Of course, even vows may not promise her that much, and that was exactly what ate at her. "Does it even matter, though?" she added petulantly.

"Does it even matter?" Michael echoed, frowning and lowering his mug. "Does *what* even matter?"

She shook her head and tried for a smile. "Nothing."

"No, what is it, Amelia? Do you mean the reception? We can try to have it at the lighthouse. Or the field. I just figured winter in Birch Harbor—it'll be freezing. Gloomy, even. You know? I mean—no one will fit in the lighthouse, and surely tents in the snow on the field won't work."

"Right, exactly." She nodded and took a deep breath. "The country club is ideal. Or we could even have something at your house."

"*Our* house," Michael chided gently.

Her chest tightened. Amelia had only just gotten settled in her own space there, next to the lighthouse. The thought of leaving it—of moving yet again—unnerved her.

CHAPTER 12—CLARA

"You spent the night at *his house*?" Megan hissed into the phone. Once Sarah fessed up, all concerns over who was driving what boat instantly fell off the radar.

"No," Clara replied, tucking the phone between her ear and shoulder as she dug deeper into the hope chest, silently praying that somehow it had magically made its way back in there. "What are you talking about?"

Megan's voice evened out. "Then where *are* you? The girls are at your house—"

"I'm in my room... at my house," Clara answered, pushing aside sleeves of doilies and feeling to the corkboard false bottom.

"Sarah said you weren't home," Megan answered, resuming her accusation.

"Well, I am. I got home at eleven, and the girls were conked out in the living room. I went out this morning at six, and they were still asleep, so I got my coffee and came back in here." She had no idea why she was defending herself. "What's up with the third degree?"

"Sorry," Megan replied. "I just had a panic attack that you and Jake were holed up in his house and left the girls alone and—" She let out an audible sigh. "—I guess I'm still a little anxious about all things Birch Harbor High."

Clara couldn't help but take it as a slight. Luckily, she was distracted enough by the distinct absence of the secret notebook that she could shrug off any sisterly implication. "Well, I'm anxious, too," she confessed, pushing up from the hope chest and repositioning the phone in her hand.

"You are? Why? Is it Judith?" Megan asked.

"Judith? What? No. It's—did Sarah mention anything about a—" Just as Clara was about to fess up entirely, one of the girls called her voice from the hall. "Oh, never mind. Megan, I have to go. The girls are fine. I've been here all night. Talk later, okay?"

She got off the phone and padded up the hall in her socks. "Everything okay out here?"

"We're about to go," Sarah swung her bag up over her shoulder as Clara's eyes landed past her, on the other three girls each lining up by the door.

"Okay," Clara's voice wobbled, and her eyes flew to the coffee table. "Let me, um, just make sure you got everything." She all but jogged to the living room, and her hands flew through the books and DVDs, her eyes darting around the sofa and the floor. But she came up empty. No secret notebook. It was gone. And not one of the girls had said anything yet. There'd been no frantic phone call from Kate or Amelia. Megan was more worried about where Clara had spent her night—as *if* she were uncouth enough to stay over at Jake's while his own daughter was in the cottage. *What*?

She shook her head and looked up at the girls, trying to meet each one's gaze. Sarah gave her a smile and started for the door, where Paige was already rattling off information about meeting someone somewhere. Mercy and Vivi were lost in a conversation of their own, whispering to each other.

Clara bit down hard on her lower lip, wincing uselessly. Was she stupid to plant it? Was she stupid to involve the girls in the business of a missing man? Someone they had so little to do with that there was no question they'd find any such discovery to be utterly irrelevant and boring.

But now, Clara didn't even have the darn thing to reveal to her sisters, anyway. If she said anything without the notebook in hand, then she'd have to confess she misplaced it. And then what?

She'd been dumb. Dumb, immature, and silly.

The girls began throwing goodbyes and thank yous and aimless waves over their shoulders as Clara racked her memory for *where* exactly she'd left it. Had she positioned it on the kitchen table? Her eyes flew there as she followed the girls out into the chilly morning air.

Nothing on the kitchen table. The coffee table. She swallowed and waved after the girls as they loaded into Paige's car, all ready to head off on their next adventure. Something about a day at the marina.

Clara pulled her sweater sleeves down over her hands and hugged herself.

Just as she was about to turn to go in and rip the house apart to find the stupid notebook that she never ought to have treated like some sort of a game... Vivi called out to her.

"Miss Hannigan!" She stood crooked inside the right rear door.

Clara frowned and took a step away from her door. "Yes?" she called back.

A moment passed, and in that moment, something flickered across the distance. Passing clouds converging together in front of the sun. A bird flapping overhead.

"Thank you!" the girl called back, her white-blonde hair whipping across her face before she slipped into the car, and they drove off, leaving Clara alone with her bad decision.

CHAPTER 13—NORA

WENDELL ACTON CASE

It's mid-November (don't ask me the date), and the search is officially postponed. Officially and perhaps indefinitely if you ask me.

Life has been... hard. Very hard. I suppose I didn't quite know just how much Wendell did for the girls and me. Now, everything falls on my shoulders, and though I don't regret how the past year has played out, I often look back to the better days of our life together.

When we returned from Arizona, I thought we could tuck away in the cottage and remain out of the public eye for some time as the town got used to the notion that there was a new Hannigan baby.

Of course, this was probably a ridiculous idea to begin with. It was made more ridiculous by Wendell's disappearance, naturally. In fact, when we returned to town, the spotlight swiveled onto my face, and Clara's downy baby hair caught it, too. Since our chance to blend in didn't exist, we had to hide instead. Flat-out hide if you can imagine.

The spotlight, however, was brief. Once people knew I was tucked away inside a muumuu, a baby strapped against my conspicuously flat chest, the town took a collective step back and whispered, "*Oooh.*"

Suddenly, the police thought they had solved the riddle of the poor, missing Wendell Acton. I found this out through Mathers, who'd initially rubbed me the wrong way. It was over an especially strained breakfast at the Harbor Deli where he had said (and I'll never forget this): *Nora, when you came home with a surprise baby, everyone's suspicions were confirmed.*

Dog tired and worried *sick*, I was confused.

He explained, *Wendell left you because you had an affair.* And he tipped his to-go coffee at the baby.

In truth, this made perfect sense.

I'm disgusted with myself, and I know better than to commit what about I'm about to commit to the page. I know better than to *feel* this way, but something occurred to me then. Either the town can *know* that Kate had a baby in high school. They can *know* my daughter's secret... or they can *think* they know mine.

CHAPTER 14—KATE

Kate and Judith had managed to avoid each other for thirty-six hours. Or maybe it was only Kate avoiding Judith. Now that Kate had finally accepted that she'd better serve and join her guest for the final breakfast, Judith was primed and ready for a conversation. Kate could sense it. The bubbling intensity of someone on a mission.

Kate opened with the question she had been wording and rewording in her mind all of Friday night and all day Saturday. "So, what really brought you to the Heirloom Inn this weekend, Judith? It's no secret you have your defenses up against my sisters and me." She lowered into a seat as Judith stabbed her eggs Benedict at the kitchen table.

"You're right." Judith met her gaze, and a grin pricked at the corners of her lips. "I made it clear I was wary of you."

Kate silently wished Matt were there with her, holding her hand beneath the table or taking ownership of the conversation and kicking this woman out for good. But she took a breath and answered, "And your behavior has made us wary of *you*."

Judith cleared her throat. "Katherine—*Kate*," she sucked in a tight breath, "I don't live here full time. That's true. But I'm from the Island, and my family founded Birch Harbor, same as yours did." Her voice softened, and she drew a slow sip of her coffee, her eyes dancing out through the window.

Kate remained quiet.

"I don't know the trouble our ancestors had together. Not firsthand. But I know the trouble my own family had when they attempted to make a life on the Island. They were outcasts. Religious zealots, to some. Misfits, effectively. Recovering from that didn't come easily, and few Bankses ever did make their way back into Birch Harbor. Some died. Some eventually left for Detroit or Chicago. Who knows? But for whatever reason, Kate, those of us who stuck around —we still didn't thrive. Not like the Hannigans or Fiorillos or Matuszewskis. We continued to struggle. My parents seemed to pass that tradition on like some sort of award, too. They considered it a merit to bear the brunt of heartache. My siblings and I—we wore trials and tribulations like Boy Scouts wear badges." She pushed air out from the thin space between her lips. "Maybe those badges turned into armor."

"Armor?" Kate interjected. "Armor for what? Against what, rather?"

Judith slid a perfect square of eggs into her mouth and chewed thoughtfully. "The threat of losing what we *did* manage to build."

"And what was that?" It wasn't a rhetorical question. Kate honestly didn't know what the Banks family had on Heirloom Island. Even when she had pressed Matt on the question, he didn't know, either. He spent the lion share of his days in town, not out there. *I just live here!* he joked when Kate spent time on Heirloom and nagged him with questions about this café or that—this business or that. Though small, Heirloom Island was like a mirror image of Birch Harbor, complete with its own clump of notable families, its own main drag and marina and eateries and even the storied school.

"Oh." Judith fluttered her eyelashes and pursed her lips, affronted apparently. "St. Mary's. Surely you knew?"

"No," Kate replied at once, frowning deeply. "The Bankses *built* St. Mary's?" She didn't understand. Certainly, Kate was no expert on all matters of the local Catholic parishes—or the diocese, for that matter. But she ought to know a simple fact such as that.

"From the ground up, yes. My great-aunt Mary was the head nun brought over from St. Patrick's to open the school while the Banks men erected the parish, the rectory and, later, the Family Hall and annex."

"Is that why..." Kate glanced at her plate then back up to Judith, whose gaze returned to the kitchen window. "Is that why you went to school there? With my mother?"

Judith turned her head. "Yes."

"Oh," Kate managed, and Judith fixed her stare once again out the window, but her eyes darted back and forth. Shaking her head, Kate went on, "I'm sorry, Judith, but I still don't understand. Why the beef with Megan's business? Why come here? Because you were forced to go to a school for troubled girls?"

She shook her head. "Two other reasons," Judith answered on a breath, swallowed audibly then looked into Kate's eyes. "Firstly, I know my husband was in love with your mother. He was until the day she died."

Confused, Kate opened her mouth to reply, but Judith held up her hand.

"It was hard on me. To see you girls return and reawaken

that interest for him—the interest in Nora and in their past." Her eyes flitted down. "In *his* past."

Kate nodded. "I can understand that. And... is that why you're here now? This weekend? To make peace or something? So we can coexist on the Lake? You and Gene. And us?"

Judith shook her head sharply. "I'm leaving him."

CHAPTER 15—CLARA

"I've made a mistake." Her voice trembled over the line.

"What kind of mistake?" Jake asked, his voice grumbly and rough. She wondered if he usually slept in, or if he was taking advantage of a morning without Mercy. Maybe he'd been awake for some time, and she just happened to be the first person he'd spoken to that morning.

Well, no. Surely, Mercy was home.

Still, Clara stole a moment to wonder what it might be like if she'd get to share a quiet, sleepy morning with Jake one day. Mercy or no Mercy, Clara would savor it.

Shaking her head, she let out a sigh. "It's a weird story, and you're definitely going to think less of me."

"Nothing you could do or not do would make me think less of you," he murmured.

She wasn't sold on that, but still. If any of the girls had uncovered the case report and squirreled it away, it would have to have been Mercy. She was shy and quiet—the only one who might feel embarrassed or nervous... but still curious. The only one like Clara, who'd want to tuck it away so that the world remained just as it was.

Clara was certain of this. She had settled on such a conclusion once she'd flipped the cottage upside down in a desperate search, only to come up empty.

Sighing more gravely this time, she launched into a careful overview of the discovery she'd made the night of Homecoming—the *Wendell Acton Case* notebook. She detailed her unease with opening the book and carrying forth the reopening of the case that Amelia and Michael had been chipping away at. Even as she confessed the fact that she had kept the notebook a secret for so long, Clara realized what a selfish and petulant thing it was to do.

"I'm foolish, I know," she said, stopping for a breath.

"It's understandable," Jake assured her. "You want to keep the past in the past. I get that."

"But I could have passed it over back then. Right away. Amelia would die to have that notebook, and I kept it from her. And maybe Kate and Megan would appreciate it, too, but I was too scared to be dragged back into the drama, and... who does that? Who isn't dying to know what happened to Wendell? All of Birch Harbor probably wonders, still. Anyone old enough, at least."

"Maybe, but now you were ready to hand it off, right?"

"Yeah, and what was I *thinking*? Leaving it for the girls to find? Expecting them to make a more mature decision than I did?"

There was a pause on the line. A beat too long.

She'd been beyond foolish. She'd acted like a child, and if there was one thing that Jake was disinterested in, it was dating someone who acted worse than his own daughter. No doubt about that.

She gave him another second to respond, and he did.

"You know what, I just—um—I'm getting another call, and—"

Her heart sank then and there, but she managed to interrupt him, "Jake, I'm sorry. I..." She shouldn't have called, is what she wanted to say. But family came first, and the least she could do now was set about righting her wrong. "Before you go, I need to talk to Mercy. I think she might have taken it."

CHAPTER 16—MEGAN

"They went to the lake," Megan told a frantic Clara over the phone. "Why? What's going on?"

It sounded like her little sister was holding back tears, and Megan's gut churned. "I hope nothing happened last night. Clara? Did something *happen*?"

"No. I don't know. I don't *think* so. It's just... Megan, I can't talk about it over the phone. Can we meet? At the Inn? I have to track them down—Mercy, especially."

"Kate has Judith there, and she said she needed—"

"I don't *care* about Judith. This is way more important. You have to trust me. Call Amelia and meet me there."

The line went dead, and Megan's jaw tensed. Still, she grabbed her keys, called goodbye to Brian, and flew out the door, dialing Amelia on the way.

∾

"THIS BETTER BE GOOD," Amelia murmured when she approached the front gate to the house. Having arrived just before Amelia, Megan had waited for her.

"I just hope there wasn't another situation with the girls."

"There wasn't." The voice came from the door. It was Clara.

Megan locked eyes as she neared her. "There *wasn't*?"

"It's a situation with me. And... *Nora*, I guess you could say."

Amelia came up behind Megan. "Is Judith still here?" As she said it, Kate appeared behind Clara in the door, all four of them present, accounted for, and sufficiently on edge.

"Yes, she is."

Megan stepped inside and craned her neck, searching the parlor and great room. "Where?" she hissed.

Kate held up her hands. "Listen, things are *delicate*."

"Delicate *bad* or delicate *good*?" Amelia prodded.

Hesitating a moment as she twisted around to glance through to the kitchen, Kate replied, "Both."

"I just need to know the girls are okay. Did they come through?" Megan started for the kitchen, and no one stopped her. The others followed.

Kate's voice came after her. "No, but we caught sight of them on the water."

"Did they seem to be okay?" Megan pressed.

"Yes?" Kate replied. "I guess. I mean—I couldn't see their expressions or anything, but they waved to us and called hello from their boat."

Megan's pulse slowed to a dull throb. "Okay." She checked her phone again, her frantic calls and texts to Sarah still sitting unreturned.

The four women moved into the kitchen, but Judith was nowhere to be seen.

"Now, listen," Kate whispered, glancing over her shoulder and off to the dining room. "I'm making progress with Judith. Long story short, I think we're at the point where bygones can be bygones with her."

Amelia replied, "What are you talking about? She doesn't hate us? We don't hate her? What—just because she threw a little money your way, or something?"

Megan spoke before Kate could answer, "Hold on. We're here because Clara called us together. Because of something to do with the *girls*, I might add."

"Not the girls," Clara snapped, then sank back on her heels. "Sorry. Not the girls—it's just..."

Kate drew a finger to the kitchen window. "There she is."

"Sarah?" Megan asked, striding to the window.

"No, Judith," Kate answered, following Megan but opening the door and stepping out into the chilly air.

"It's freezing out there. I knew I should have told them *no*." Megan followed Kate, rubbing her hands up and down her arms as Clara and Amelia stepped out behind her.

Outside, Megan squinted through the sun, searching the marina and then the water that spread out from the back of the Inn. No boat came into sight.

"Judith!" Kate called down to the beach, and only then did Megan's eyes narrow in on the frail, blonde-headed woman who stood at the south corner of the property. But it wasn't Judith's form that her gaze froze upon.

It was the object at which the woman was pointing—a boat in the distance, past the cove and across the bay.

Four pairs of arms had shot up into the air, waving frantically.

From her distance, even moving toward them, down through the seawall and onto the sand, Megan couldn't ascertain if one of the pairs was Sarah's or not, but she knew there ought to be five pairs.

Sarah, Mercy, Vivi, Paige, and Paige's older sister.

Five pairs of arms.
Not four.

CHAPTER 17—NORA

WENDELL ACTON CASE

I've thought hard about the consequences of each of my two options.

If I come clean about Kate's teenage pregnancy, the search *could* heat back up. *Maybe.*

In fact, when I tested this theory and protested the allegations of the affair and *assured* Mathers that the baby was mine and Wendell's, Mathers said it was a moot point.

A missing middle-aged man of good health and with no known enemies was at the bottom of a long list of the county's concerns. Especially when that man's wife left for the summer and returned with a new child. And *especially* when friends of the family reported to the police that they had no recollection of seeing me with a growing belly, but they *did* recall that I pulled Kate, Amelia, and Megan from school early the previous spring. Of course, they seemed to conveniently forget the last-minute, intimate shower I fibbed about at church and around Birch Harbor. They seemed to forget all those miniature measures I thoughtfully took to make a modest announcement—something in line with what a woman of a certain age might do if she found herself in the position of a late-in-life baby.

And then, on Halloween night, when a little girl went missing just south of town, Wendell fell off the radar. All search efforts were instantly redirected to the truer tragedy —a lost child. There was no way I would tug attention from that, anyhow.

Interest stalled out in Wendell and me and our new, suspicious baby. And by now, the world has forgotten about him, and they have forgotten about me and Clara and now —it seems they believe that Baby Clara really is Wendell's. And perhaps *that* was the reason he left. It's funny how memories shape around new rumors and squeeze out old ones.

That's all to say that revealing Kate's secret may or may not have much of an impact by now.

As for allowing everyone to believe that I had an affair, and the new baby wasn't Wendell's—well, technically the only person who could get hurt was me. And if such an untruth were to reemerge, I could fight back and rise above. I could reverse it all.

Kate could hardly do such a thing, and I've been where she is. I know the impact it could have—how it could keep her from true love. How it could threaten her wedding day like my secret threatened mine. And even now, in this modern age with these modern morals, there's no telling what sort of mother-in-law lurks in the shadows.

CHAPTER 18—AMELIA

What happened next was all a blur. Megan screamed back to call 911 before sprinting across the sand and toward the bay. "*One is missing!*" she added, her voice pure panic.

Judith dashed back up, and Kate dashed down, following Megan.

Clara starting crying that she didn't have her phone, *she didn't have her phone*. Amelia fumbled her own out of her back pocket as she, Clara, and Judith jogged through the house to the street to clamber into Clara's car.

Amelia instructed the operator to send help to Birch Bay —there'd been an accident with teenagers and a boat.

Of course, back at the house, when she'd screened the sun from her eyes and peered as precisely as she could, she had surmised that there was no *obvious* accident. Still, Megan and Kate would know—they were the mothers of the group. They had the intuition, the *sense* that *something* was going on. Something horrible.

Clara white-knuckled the steering wheel, careening up

Harbor Avenue as Judith remained chillingly silent in her seat in the front.

Amelia called Michael next, her voice pinched as she held back her panic.

"Where are they?" he asked.

"The bay. It looks like they're out on the bay."

"What bay?" he asked, and she could hear him moving purposefully around her house, where she'd left him just a half hour earlier on a different, less serious but equally vague urgency.

"Birch Bay," she hissed back, unnecessarily impatient. "Down past St. Patrick's."

"I'm on my way," he replied. "Have you called Matt? Jake?"

Amelia winced. It would have made more sense if she had. "No, no. I—I don't know what to do."

"I'll take care of it and meet you there."

"Okay," Amelia replied. "Thanks, Michael. Thank you."

She clutched her phone mercilessly in her hand. "I don't know why I didn't call Jake. Or Matt. I'm sorry, Clara," Amelia whimpered.

"Who's Michael?" Judith's voice came soft and in stark contrast to her formidable reputation among the Hannigan women.

Amelia's knee-jerk reaction was to tell her to shut up. Mind her business. Jump out a window. But she took a breath and answered, "Michael Matuszewski."

"He's my lawyer," Judith revealed quietly.

Taken aback, Amelia simply echoed her, "He's your lawyer?"

"Yes. Well. He *was*. Gene's lawyer. Maybe that means he's not mine anymore. Is he yours, too?"

Amelia saw Clara steal a glance at Judith, amazed at the

woman's ability to formulate either small talk or complete aloofness to all the happenings in the Hannigans' lives. Perhaps Clara, like Amelia, was confused. What could it mean that Michael was Gene's lawyer but no longer Judith's lawyer?

"Michael is my fiancé," Amelia answered coolly as Clara turned sharply onto a sandy access road that ran parallel to the lake. They were almost there.

Judith looked back at Amelia, and a genuine smile lifted her face. "He's a good man. You're lucky, Amelia."

Amelia twitched at Judith's familiar use of her name. The compliment. The bizarreness of everything.

Still, she managed to respond, "I know."

And Amelia did know that Michael was a good man. And she did know that she was lucky, and she knew that even in her discomfort with planning a wedding and committing to one life—there in Birch Harbor, the place she'd run from for so long—she knew that the running from things was over.

Clara threw her car into park. Amelia burst out the door and ran down the beach and straight out to the water. She stopped short before wading in and shielded her eyes from the sun, squinting past a floating buoy and to the girls' boat.

Two of them were still waving, the other three out of sight or hidden by the glare of the morning sun.

But it wasn't the girls Amelia narrowed her focus on. It was the object of their frantic pointing—the dock at St. Patrick's.

At the piling furthest out, something poked out from the wood, a round bunch of twigs, like an oversized nest, almost.

Amelia squinted hard as she resumed jogging—up to the church property, down the sidewalk, and through the seawall—until her gaze leveled on the protrusion and the fact that the girls were now tying themselves off.

And there were five girls. All safe.

All excited over what looked to be nothing more than a dead wreath coiled around a wooden cross. Hidden deep inside the grape vines of the wreath, there was a crude inscription.

From Nora. To Wendell. Dated just the winter before.

CHAPTER 19—KATE

After dismissing the police and calling Matt back to apologize for the scare, Kate finally had a moment to catch her breath and join the madness on the dock. She would have been embarrassed that they had caused such a fuss, except Kate knew just how treacherous a body of water *could* be. Seeing just the four pairs of hands waving wildly—the boat veering in the opposite direction as Megan had sprinted alongside the water and down the shore... the only logical conclusion she might draw was that there was a problem. And if they'd been too late to act—if they'd stopped for a moment to stare harder or juggle with their cell phones and the spotty service to call one of the girls—the fleeting chance of a rescue may have passed. Their lives might have been changed forever.

That sort of thing had happened to Kate before. In fact, when it had come to life-changing moments, she'd had her share. First with learning about Clara—the little life inside her. Then with Wendell. And thereafter, with all of those ordinary milestones that weren't so ordinary when they happened to you. Marriage. More children. *Raising* those children. Then losing her mother.

Kate hadn't been to St. Patrick's or its little bay since her mother's funeral.

Small and brief, the service had been memorable but simple—a classy cremation as opposed to a drawn-out procession and hearse and lowering of the casket. Kate had been surprised that Nora had preferred a cremation over something more classic—but then again, perhaps cremation was en vogue of late. Nora would have known. She'd have researched it until the very end.

Smiling to herself, Kate recalled quite clearly that they had arrived at the church, lingered fleetingly in front, entered, sat for the Mass, wept in waves, and then left out the front with the funeral director—who then transported the ashes to the cemetery the next day for the burial. Not once did Kate or her sisters loiter by the water like other funeral attendees. Not once did Kate go to the dock. She was far too absorbed in other things.

And she hadn't been back there since then, shamefully. Something about St. Patrick's had warded her off. A faith crisis? No. Kate was most certainly a believer. She said her prayers. She believed. It was... *everything else*. Excuses about the busy world of running an around-the-clock business. Discomfort in her arrangement with Matt, perhaps— though it didn't feel uncomfortable. It felt the opposite. Quite comfortable. Perhaps they'd legalize it, after all. Maybe that would give her a little peace of mind? That she wasn't playing house at the ripe old age of... well...

And then, most prominently, existed that edgy memory of the day when she had posed in front of a dark-stained rosewood box and lots and *lots* of flowers. The smell of roses, indeed, had stained her brain.

So, St. Patrick's could sit there against the far southern cove of town and wait for the day when Kate got over it. When she could officially move on from the pain surrounding her mother... *and* her father.

And anyway, it was easy enough for a local to avoid a place like Birch Bay.

In the summer, the sandy curve was overrun with tourists looking for the perfect sunbathing spot. In the winter, well, suffice it to say, no one dared dip a toe in Lake Huron. Not even in the fall or spring, really, was it an enjoyable experience. The only souls one might find on the bay on a Sunday were churchgoers (and maybe Kate would one day be that again—a staunch churchgoer. She'd like to, at least).

Anyway, it was nearing noon, and the place was dead.

That's why it made no sense to see a boatful of girls waving excitedly, slowly motoring across the lake, their destination confusing to Kate and unmooring to the others, clearly.

Now Kate stood with her sisters and the well-meaning bunch of teenagers as everyone stared at the wreath.

"Did you bring her out to do this, Clara?" Amelia asked.

Clara hung in the back, wary, it seemed. "No. I didn't know she came out here at all. And she wasn't driving, so I also don't know *how* she got here."

Kate glanced toward the front of the church, where Judith had wandered off to.

At St. Patrick's, Sunday Mass was offered at seven o'clock and nine o'clock, and it appeared as though they had stumbled into the bay after the post-Mass exodus.

The dock at St. Patrick's sat perennially empty. Father Vann was too old to make much use of the diocese-issued boat that sat rusting in a shed out back. Heirloom Island had its own parish, and there was nothing particularly special about this one that drove boaters in. Only by accident or a sense of adventure would someone purposefully come to dock there.

Kate squeezed her eyes shut, exhausted from the buildup of anxiety over Judith's stay at the Inn and still recovering from her panic that one of the girls had been injured or fallen overboard.

Now, with five girls accounted for, four sisters present, four men en route, and one brittle stranger hovering near the Mary Magdalene statue, Kate could try to focus on the discovery.

She reached for the card that Amelia held and read it to herself, desperate to rekindle the memory of Nora's voice to make sense of it all.

But when she fixed her eyes on the words—the few words in the now-familiar script of a woman with a thousand secrets or more—they rang empty.

Or did they?

After three reads in her head, she tested the sentence aloud, focusing not on the two names—Dear Wendell... All my love, Nora—or the date. Focusing strictly on the message.

"I'll see you soon," Kate whispered.

"What does that mean?" Sarah asked.

Kate turned on a heel. "Wait a minute."

The others took a collective step back. "What?" Megan asked, her arms still clutched around Sarah's waist.

"What brought you here? Why did you come out here?"

The question was meant for all five of the girls, but it was Vivi who stepped forward, a black notebook gripped in her small, thin fingers.

She didn't offer it to Kate, though. Instead, she held it tightly against her chest and turned to face to Clara.

"We found something in Miss Hannigan's cottage."

CHAPTER 20—NORA

WENDELL ACTON CASE

Christmas is looming, and I've yet to document much lately. The only thing to write, I suppose, is that I finally mustered the courage to call Detective Mathers.

Things went as well as I'd hoped they would—or better —and what strikes me now, as I jot this down, is just how visceral an experience this has all turned into. Back in the summer, I might have just listed off the fragments of information I had—and all of that was soulless and sinewy at best.

Now, I have a broader picture of this town and my place in it. Sometimes I feel like I'm watching a movie—like I'm watching myself rush through the days to arrive at the empty nights. I'm watching myself wait for the next juncture where I'll have a moment to flee the girls and follow a lead. But, you see, I keep it from them. Our lives are already made more complicated. Filling the free moments with talk of our shared tragedy would do none of them any good.

I've stopped humoring Amelia's unrelenting inquisition into the fate of her father. I've ignored Kate's passive-aggressive notions about flipping the script and airing our laundry. I've buried it all. Here, in this notebook, is the only place I'll give it any attention outside of my personal diary. Otherwise, our lives would be utterly consumed, and we'd get nowhere. *Nowhere.*

Anyway, when I asked Mathers about meeting me at the cottage, or even somewhere in the shadows along the marina... his attitude shifted. He melted a little, and his voice came in a reply so soaked in pity, I started to see the truth.

That he couldn't help me find Wendell.

Even so, he offered small hope. Said he wouldn't meet me anywhere. Instead, I could come to his house in the woods.

He'd show me what information he *did* have.

CHAPTER 21—CLARA

Just as the words slipped from Vivi's lips, waves kicked up, sending the rental boat bobbing high and pulling everyone's attention from the black notebook to the incoming boater.

Jake.

"What in the world is going on?" The words crashed from his mouth as the boat drifted to a stop just short of the far end of the dock. Jake scrambled to knot his rope around the piling and hopped onto the wooden landing, but Mercy had already taken off, running to meet him before Clara could even check to see whether he'd responded to her text that it was a false alarm.

"Dad, everyone's fine! We found something to help Miss Hannigan and her sisters. We found something!" Mercy's voice turned winded as she ran down the dock and grabbed her dad's hand to drag him back.

"Clara? What's going on. I thought somebody *died*."

Clara jogged, too, meeting them both at the edge of the dock. "I'm so sorry, Jake. We thought there was an emergency.

Judith—" She swung a useless arm off toward the front of the church and as she did, she took in the faces of the others. Vivi's silken hair streaming back against a breeze, Sarah's hand over her eyes, staring back. And Paige and her sister's blank ones. Kate, Amelia, and Megan huddled against the cold, waiting.

Clara crossed one arm across her stomach, stilling the nausea that crept in. Her evening with Jake passed through her mind.

His cozy cabin in the woods—dinner, dessert, and a movie. Their fifth and most special date, in her eyes. The one that led them to bigger conversations—more serious talk. The future, short and long term. The past—his difficult and full; hers simple and hollow. Then her mind retraced their fleeting conversation that very morning. The one when she had confessed her ridiculous plot to entrap the girls and shake off the unearthed secret that belonged not to any of them, but to Clara and her sisters. His cool response—a supposed phone call. Her determination to make things right and talk to Mercy, only to learn that Mercy wasn't home. Of course she wasn't. She was out in the boat with the others, merrymaking and adventuring across Lake Huron like the gang from Scooby Doo.

"Can we all... go somewhere and talk?" Clara managed.

"I have to get back to the marina," Jake answered. "I got a call this morning about a faulty buoy. I was just about to head out there when I got your text." He didn't meet Clara's eyes.

Something felt familiar about the excuse. *Was* it an excuse? Was it the truth? Was Jake trying to shake her off, or was there *actually* a faulty buoy?

"Come on, Dad. Let someone else handle it."

"No one else *can* handle it, Mercy." Jake pushed a hand

through his hair, then braced it on his daughter's shoulder. "Are you okay? What *happened*?"

Mercy's gaze flew to Clara who passed it off on the others as they watched with interest the little dance between the trio on the dock.

Clara ran her tongue over her bottom lip, and, out of the corner of her eye, she spotted Judith wandering back.

"We thought something had happened, but we were wrong. Everything's okay. I'm sorry I scared you, but Jake, you can go. You can go back to the marina," Clara said, accepting that she had two purposes. One: Get the notebook into the right hands. Two: Prove to Jake she wasn't some nutjob teacher who couldn't face her own problems—she was a grown woman who could *solve* them.

The thing she needed to do above all else—regardless of whether it meant a difference in Jake's sudden change in attitude—still sat before her. She needed to tear that stupid notebook out of Vivi's hands and stab a finger at every page until they had all the answers to all their questions.

The only problem was Clara had no idea what was in that notebook. For all she knew, Nora had simply written something obscure about the church and that's what had drawn the girls out there.

Clara had no idea if the notebook was any more useful.

Because Clara herself hadn't even cracked it open.

Her fear was too great. What if there was no answer? She'd have disappointed Amelia. What if the answer was bigger than their expectations? Wendell was alive and well, living out in the sticks, undercover and off the grid? Maybe he *didn't* love his family. Maybe he *had* run from them?

Clara knew what that kind of a betrayal could do to a person. She had seen it in her students when their parents got a divorce and one picked up with a new family else-where. Kids wrote about that kind of thing—taking to their faintly lined composition books to document their grief, to seek out some form of relief.

Life was now going well for Kate, Amelia, and Megan —*and* Clara, hopefully. To learn that Wendell had done exactly what the town thought he did—what the Actons themselves thought he did—could bring them back to zero. It might remind Amelia of the comfort of being on the road and not ever committing to one spot. It might remind Megan to be a little more wary of her own marriage.

What if Wendell left because of Kate's condition? Because of... Clara herself? Had her own existence been the single deciding factor?

"No, wait, Dad." Mercy propped her hands on her waist. "You can't go."

Jake let out a sigh, his gaze landing briefly on Clara, who saw something there—a chill or a question... disappointment?

"Why not, Mercy?" He held up a straight finger. "And think about this, because you'll be keeping me from making an urgent marina repair."

Though his words were coated thickly in guilt, Mercy stood her ground. "Mathers, Dad."

He cocked his head. "Mathers? What about Mathers?"

"Mom's father. Clint Mathers. He was the detective in Wendell Acton's disappearance. Did you know that?"

Clara's eyes grew wide, and she looked over her shoulder to see if the others were listening carefully. Their furrowed brows and squinting eyes revealed nothing. "What are you talking about, Mercy?" she asked.

The girl drew her finger across the dock to where the others stood. "It's all in the notebook. All this information about Clara's dad's case. That's why we came here. She wrote about the church and the bay and how he was last seen working on his boat. I think we can figure it out."

Jake's face softened. "Mercy," he began, but she shook her head sharply.

"No, Dad. This is *important*. And my own *ancestors* were involved. Maybe it mattered to them. Maybe it had to do with why they left town to begin with."

Jake lifted his stare to Clara, setting his jaw in place before looking out to the lake.

"And you need *me* for this?" Even as he said it, Clara heard that the question wasn't for Mercy. And it wasn't a question. It was a statement. For *her*.

"No."

Frowning, he parted his lips as if to reply, but Mercy started in again on her begging. Clara held up a hand to each.

"Jake, you should go fix the buoy," Clara instructed. "Mercy, he can meet us later. Okay?"

She shook her head. "We *do* need him," she wailed.

"Why?" Clara and Jake asked at once, and for half a second, they could have been a serious couple—the kind they had talked about being. They could have been a married couple, even, teamed up against any parent's greatest opponent: a stubborn child.

"So he can take us to the lighthouse."

"We can drive to the lighthouse, Mercy," Clara reasoned. "And what's there, anyway?"

Mercy shook her head. "That's not our plan. We're going to retrace Nora's footsteps. We need to be on the water."

Jake looked at Clara, pleading in his eyes.

"How about this, Mercy?" she answered, sucking in a breath. "Your dad can go fix the buoy and when he's done, he can meet us back at the house on the harbor."

"Okay, fine," Mercy said, her voice pinched. "But not at the house on the harbor. You'll have to come wherever we are by then." She crossed her arms and lifted her eyebrows to her father.

"Let's just plan on the house," Clara tried again, distinctly uncomfortable with a family pow-wow at St. Patrick's.

But Mercy shook her head. "You don't understand. Nora said to start *here*."

CHAPTER 22—NORA

WENDELL ACTON CASE

I got home late last night. Too late. Kate had to put Clara down, and Amelia and Megan were starving. For food or attention or both, I don't know.

Their basic needs came first, so after a long night of baking cookies and promising them that *yes,* everything was okay and *no,* I didn't have new information—just a dinner with friends (that's what I said), I was too tired to return here and document what I learned. The good thing, though, was that I have all I need now.

Here's what happened.

Yesterday afternoon, I headed deep into the backwoods of town and down a winding, snow-packed road.

With snow and ice so treacherous, I'd have guessed it was mid-February already. But it isn't. Icicles dangled from trees as I turned down a nameless frosted lane. I remember thinking that maybe Mathers wasn't the useless, kindly ol' detective I thought he was. Maybe I'd be kidnapped and taken to wherever they were keeping Wendell...

But then, I arrived at this white-blanketed cabin, a strip of Christmas lights glowing along the eaves, and I remembered there *was* something left in the year. And here I was, so burdened with my own choices, I'd have nearly washed the season right out with my grief and fears.

Mathers and his wife ushered me inside, and I learned immediately what clutter bugs they both were. I could hardly step a foot inside without bumping into this set of drawers or that—and a whole pack of hunting dogs squeezed in and out through the single narrow path that veered around the cramped quarters.

I sat uncomfortably at their kitchen table, and that's where Detective Mathers spread three files out for my benefit.

He began by making small talk over the lost little girl— found just four days after Halloween (praise God). The small talk veered into the tedium of daily life in his job until he finally cut to the chase.

Wendell's case was suspended due to a variety of factors: funding to the department was cut; Mathers was reassigned out of his detective title, and no one was hired to replace him; local rumors held fast.

I needn't have asked what the local rumors were, but still I did. I have a mystery to solve, and I need all available information.

Mathers confirmed again what I still didn't want to believe: everyone felt certain that Wendell had refused to tolerate whatever my delicate condition meant. My "indiscretion," was the word he used.

Instead of arguing about the point, I pulled out this very notebook and pressed my finger against my musings and the information I had gleaned from the Actons.

In reply, he took me carefully through every last piece of evidence they had uncovered.

In the end, we clasped our hands neatly over our respective pages, met each other's gaze, and came to the empty realization that there was nothing more to know.

And that's why tonight, I'm changing tactics. Instead of thinking and reflecting and calling all the wrong people, it's time I call the right ones.

Since this town is dead set on the probability of my having something to do with it, I'll start at the beginning.

And if anyone else should ever recover this notebook... and if, by then, Wendell is still lost... I hope that you will go there, too. To where our lives began: St. Patrick's.

And when you get there, you'll know who to ask for and what to do.

CHAPTER 23—SARAH

Clara and Mercy made their way back to where Sarah and the others waited impatiently. Sarah wanted to open her mouth and spill *everything*, but Megan told her to keep it zipped until they could all come back together. As a group.

Keeping one eye on the nervous-acting Mrs. Carmichael and one eye on Vivi and the notebook, Sarah wondered at what point one of the adults would disinvite the old lady from the family drama. Then again, they'd also have to kick Paige and her sister out. And Mercy and Mr. Hennings, too? They weren't technically part of the family, no matter how serious things were between Aunt Clara and Mr. Hennings.

"Okay," Clara declared. "We need to talk."

Sarah lifted a triumphant eyebrow at her mother who ignored her.

Instead, Megan replied, "Now? Here?"

"No," Aunt Kate answered. "We'll go back to the Inn."

"Actually," Aunt Clara interrupted. "There's somewhere else we need to go. But I think we should just start here."

"What do you mean start here?" Sarah's mom asked.

Sarah enjoyed her confoundment and exchanged a sly smile with Vivi.

When, the night before, Vivi had slid the notebook out from beneath her sleeping bag and whispered sneakily that there was something they needed to see... the game was on.

The girls had stayed up well past midnight, devouring every last detail and designing their own theories—pausing and feigning sleep when Aunt Clara's headlights had washed them in warm light.

Finally, around two in the morning, they had rested their case and agreed to head straight to "the beginning" come morning. They just needed a good excuse to get out there, and, knowing her mother, Sarah knew the best excuse would be a potential romantic connection for one of the girls.

Mercy had wanted to tell someone that they had found the notebook. *Surely, she didn't* want *us to find it*, she'd whined.

But Vivi and Sarah had protested. If Clara or any of the other adults had had their hands on that notebook (and obviously they must have; why else would it be casually lodged between *Teen Time* and *GOSSIP*), then they'd done all they could.

It was obvious that the Hannigan sisters needed a fresh set of eyes on an old case. So, that's when Sarah had declared that they would follow her grandmother's footsteps through time.

Then, that morning, when they had spotted Kate and Aunt Clara on the beach behind the Inn, their excitement had gotten the best of them, and they had begun waving frantically—gesturing to meet them on the bay. Paige's sister was focused on driving and also vaguely confused about the whole mission.

They didn't plan to give up their hunt so quickly, but apparently, the adults had panicked. And by the time they all met up where the sand turned to dock behind the old Catholic church, it was too late. It was time for everyone to have a good, old-fashioned sit down.

It sounded like Mercy had already revealed one clue, however. That they were exactly where they needed to be. Now, they just had to figure out who to ask for. And what to do.

CHAPTER 24—AMELIA

Jake Hennings had left on his boat—something about a marina repair. Vivi talked to Matt on the phone and confirmed all was well.

Paige and her sister left, too, taking their parents' boat back to the marina and telling Sarah and the other girls they'd catch up at school.

Michael, apparently, had nothing much better to do than drive down to the church. Amelia had mixed feelings about this.

On one hand, they had more than enough company to keep things interesting. Would he get in the way?

On the other hand, she liked his presence—it calmed her.

When he arrived, Kate had set about hunting down Father Vann and asking if he minded if they spent a little time in the Family Hall.

There, Sarah and her two friends pushed the black notebook to the center of the table, each clasping her hands neatly on her lap.

Creepy, if you asked Amelia.

But no one did, and she chose to loiter by the front door and wait for Michael while Megan and Clara sat with the girls, their gazes heavy on the black rectangle of truth—as Amelia considered it.

Kate stood with Amelia, waiting for Judith to finish her conversation with the priest.

"Are you going to tell her to leave?" Amelia asked.

"I can't just tell her to leave. I mean... she's the reason we're here, kind of," Kate answered.

"Because she saw the girls?"

"Mhm."

"I could have Michael drive her back to the Inn." Amelia asked as she sized the woman up. Impeccably styled and casual in her demeanor, Judith Carmichael was the epitome of small-town high society.

As the words left her mouth, Judith swiveled to them, leaving the priest to head back to the rectory while she tugged her wrap around her shoulders and returned to the door where Amelia and Kate stood.

"I know this isn't my business," Judith started, "what's happened with your mother and father, I mean."

Amelia pressed her lips into a line, and Kate let out a soft sigh. "It probably was once upon a time, though."

Frowning, Amelia shifted her weight and threw a sidelong glance at her sister.

Judith squinted. "Pardon?"

"Judith, you were on the Island when our dad went missing, right? In 1992?"

Judith replied with a curt nod. "That's right. I was at St. Mary's. Teaching."

"Maybe you can help," Kate said, waving her hand toward the long folding table where, only a half hour earlier, remnants of Sunday doughnuts and coffee sat for those parishioners who liked to linger after Mass.

"Help?" Amelia and Judith said together at once. They exchanged an awkward smile over the jinx, and Amelia lowered her voice. "Help with what, Kate?"

"Whatever is in that." Kate pointed to the table and Megan and Clara and the girls and... the notebook.

"I'm sure I can't," Judith protested, holding her palms up and taking a cautious step back. "I'm... I'm sorry, Kate." She nodded at Amelia. "Amelia. I can wait in the vestry or go for a walk or—"

"It's freezing out. Come on." Kate led the way, and Amelia and Judith had little choice but to follow.

"Okay, Sarah, Vivi, and Mercy," Kate began as she lowered herself into a white plastic chair on the other side of Clara. "What did Nora tell you?"

CHAPTER 25—MEGAN

"And when you get there, you'll know who to ask for and what to do," Megan repeated thoughtfully.

"Should we get Father Vann?" Amelia asked, searching over her shoulder.

Kate shook her head. "He wasn't the priest back then."

"But he knew Mom," Clara tried. "He knew Nora."

Megan caught the hitch in her voice and wondered if this wasn't all still a complete fool's errand. Hunting down Wendell as though he *wanted* to be found. Then again, they did have this notebook. That coupled with Nora's scattered journal entries must have added up to *something*. But what, she didn't know. The truth? Hardly. A search? Maybe. A reason for all the tears and anger and hardness in the years after that one fateful summer? Maybe.

Sarah replied, "If you read on," she began, "you'll see. I don't think it was a priest."

"Then why did you girls decide to start *here*?" Megan asked, genuinely confused.

There was a domino effect as Mercy looked at Vivi, then

Vivi looked at Sarah, who pulled the book to herself, twisted it to face the four sisters, then pushed it back.

And with that, the four sisters leaned in and read.

AFTER THE FIRST seven pages of non-information (as Megan decided to coin the ramblings of a heartbroken woman she'd never *quite* known), they leaned back.

"She was crushed," Kate remarked. "Obsessed, maybe?"

"If she were obsessed, then she would have spoken more about it when we were kids. I don't remember her ever talking about Dad," Megan answered.

"She did a little bit," Amelia revealed.

"What did she say?" Kate asked. "Because I'm with Megan, I guess. I mean... I just don't remember it being a big deal with her. With us, yes. I mean, it's all we talked about until I left for college. Right?"

"Yeah, *we* were obsessed. Especially when Amelia and I went back to school and everyone was asking us about it. I mean until I left Birch Harbor, it was all people had to say to me. 'What happened to your dad?' Like I knew? Like any of us knew."

Amelia's eyes lifted to the front doors. Megan turned to see Michael enter. When she looked back, Amelia was already leaving her chair and striding across the linoleum floor to greet him. Megan smiled to herself, wondering how their marriage prep class went—what kinds of things the priest asked—where life could take late-in-life soulmates like Amelia and Michael.

Judith cleared her throat at the far end of the table. "I remember when the news about your father hit the Island."

Megan frowned at the woman. Why was Judith

Carmichael there, and what was *wrong* with her? "Yeah, *everyone* remembers. But that means diddly squat, I guess." She crossed her arms and jutted her chin to the notebook. "If the closest person in the world to Wendell couldn't figure it out—and the police couldn't figure out—do any of you really think *we* can figure it out?"

Amelia returned with Michael at her side. "It was him," she announced, her hand crooked in his elbow.

"Huh?" Megan asked before exchanging a look with Sarah.

"Michael brought Mom to the church. Last winter. Before she got worse."

All eyes shifted to Michael as he dropped into the last free chair. "I didn't tell you because I was her lawyer at the time. I wondered where the line was with Nora—what was lawyer business and what wasn't. So, by the end, everything became confidential. You know?"

"Did she say anything then?" Megan asked, her stomach churning at the thought of her mother relying on a veritable stranger to help her with something so intimate. She licked her lips and frowned at the table.

He rubbed a hand over his mouth, his face somber and strained, like he was carrying the weight of the world. "She told me about their wedding. All about it, actually."

"It had to have mattered," Sarah jumped in, her eyes brightening at Michael's comment.

"What are you talking about?" Megan asked.

"Look," Sarah said, flipping the notebook to the next page and pushing her finger down. "This is where she started."

CHAPTER 26—NORA

WENDELL ACTON CASE

Today, I went to the church. I spoke with the Deacon and asked if he knew where Father Bart had gone.

He's been dead for eight years, I learned.

It makes no difference anyway, because there was no answer to be had at St. Patrick's. Not at Lookout Point or on the bay or the dock or the outcropping of rocks where I sat and contemplated the fact that Wendell's mother did not approve of our marriage. At least, she did not approve of Wendell marrying me.

Still, there I was, with Baby Clara bundled in my arms as we stood and watched the water lap against the dock. Winter on the lake doesn't see those lazy waves of summer. In fact, in case you didn't know, from the outcropping all the way past Lookout Point, ice forms. This doesn't always happen early in winter, and sometimes it doesn't happen at all. But today I saw that it was near, and there was a foreboding in that. The threat of the lake icing over. A way to lock secrets in and keep people out, is how I saw it.

Clara started to cry, and I bounced her up and down and returned to the car, bending low and awkward to navigate her into the little car seat. So different these days—how children are raised—padded and prodded and latched and belted so that they scarcely can explore the world. No wonder I see young mothers show up to rent a bungalow and the first thing they ask about is fenced yards this and child locks that. Neurotic, all of it. Maybe by virtue of the fact that I'm an older mother—*mother, hm*—I'll raise Clara with a different set of values all together. Perhaps she'll be scrappy. She'll face the world without fear, and she'll live life on her own terms. Not under the shadow of some moral mistake. Who knows?

Before I left the church, I drove back to the front, my tires crunching over that new snow—the Christmas kind of snow that everyone prays for. I opened the door, leaned into the crack, and studied the statute.

As a girl, I always wondered why St. Patrick's would choose Mary Magdalene of all biblical figures. The one no woman aspired to be. The wretch and the harlot. I wondered even harder why not St. Patrick himself. And then I prayed. I prayed for answers and for closure. I prayed Wendell would come back. Even if it was from the dead— I'd take him. Mainly, though, I prayed for peace. And before I left, I looked up at her—at that mirror image of me—and I still didn't understand.

Why her?

CHAPTER 27—CLARA

Clara let out a sigh and looked up after she finished reading.

Judith blinked back at her. "I know why."

All eyes turned to Judith. "You *do*?" Amelia asked.

She nodded. "My family sort of aligned with those types —the scourges. They wanted to tell that story on the Island."

"What story?" Clara asked softly.

"The story of the woman maligned. The man slandered. We were the Island of Misfits, you know."

Vivi frowned. "There's no statue of Mary Magdalene at St. Mary's, though. Our parish is named for Mother Mary, not Mary Magdalene."

"Yes, very good, dear," Judith agreed, her finger uncurling into place in front of her face. "We gifted the Mary Magdalene to St. Patrick's as a sort of truce. Early on. Maybe the forties?"

"But Nora didn't know that?" Michael blinked. "That seems improbable. She was devout. She'd have known everything."

"Not in 1992, she wasn't devout," Kate pointed out. "She didn't become that way until years later. I mean yes, she went to church. She did it all, but she wasn't as invested back then."

"But she *went* to St. Mary's," Clara reasoned, and her gaze flew to Judith. "Did you know her then?"

Judith's face remained impassive. "Hardly. Your mother was only there for a spell. For her *season*, as the nuns said. Then she left, and that was it. We didn't share classes, you see."

"Did you know—" Clara pinned a meaningful look on the woman, "—that she was there *with child*?"

Judith smiled, and her expression broke loose. "I had a feeling, but we were conditioned to be tight lipped, you see. Girls came and went at St. Mary's, usually without pomp or circumstance, if you know what I mean. That was just *life*. And they came for many reasons, too. Runaways. Drinkers. Orphans. In the sixties, we had an entire bunk dedicated to a half-dozen orphan girls."

"You mean it *wasn't* a school for young mothers?" Michael asked.

Judith shook her head. "It was a school for those who *needed* a mother. That was the saying, at least."

"Nora had a mother," Kate replied. "Gran Hannigan. Gran died when we were little, though. But that doesn't exactly explain anything. Like we, she thought to start *here*, of all places."

Shrugging, Judith let her smile slip away. "My guess is that she came *here*, to St. Patrick's, first, to think. Talk to God, maybe? She needed someone, and she had no one." Her shoulders slumped forward, and Clara felt they were getting a glimpse behind the curtain into Judith Carmichael.

Which, Clara still didn't quite understand why she was around.

"Judith," Clara began. "Why..." Her eyes darted to Kate and then to the table where she pressed her hands next to the bottom of the notebook, "I mean to say... do you *know* something about what happened to our dad? Is that why you turned up at the Inn? Is that why you're here?"

CHAPTER 28—NORA

WENDELL ACTON CASE

GOOD NEWS.

Christmas has come and gone, and baby Clara is no longer a newborn. Gone, too, are the sleepless nights. Sleepless from the early days of bringing Baby home *and* sleepless from the wire in my mind about Wendell.

I sat with my thoughts quite a while after reading my last entry here, and I did set out to make my interviews. I wanted to begin with the man who married us. I wanted to confront him and ask him how he could do that? How he could let that selfish woman intervene in our perfect day?

But it isn't Father Bart with whom I have beef. It's Wendell's mother.

There's little point in chasing her down, because I've come to understand, through word of mouth, that my little secret wasn't so secretive.

I learned that Wendell's mother knew about my teenage pregnancy. That's why she stood against us on that day so long ago. That's why she *knows* Wendell left.

But the thing of it is, I know with certainty that whatever

his mother found out or believed to be true... Wendell did not.

You see, I've just gotten off the phone with Miss Banks of St. Mary's of the Isle. Oh yes, Miss Banks. A former school-mate, Judith.

She <u>saw</u> Wendell.

CHAPTER 29—KATE

"What does this *mean*?" Her eyes were wild, voice loud, Kate braced the table and read the last line again. "And why didn't she explain it?" She pointed at the line and then at Judith. "Is Clara right? Is this why you came to the Inn? Were you... *in* on something?"

"I don't know why she didn't explain," Judith answered, her face crinkling and hands wringing.

"*You* talked to our mother? About our father? In *1993*?" Kate pressed. She didn't have patience for games, and she didn't have tolerance for whatever Judith was trying to pull over on them.

"Wait, no, no. *No*. I... I... it was *complicated*." Judith closed her eyes and pressed the pads of her fingers over the thin skin of her eyelids. "I didn't come to the Inn because of any of this—there is *nothing* new to share. Honestly, girls." She opened her eyes again, and they shone—bleary and dreadful. "There is *nothing* new for me to tell you. It's *not* why I came."

"Then why did you?" Kate pointed a finger, fierce and unhinged. "And why are you divorcing Gene?"

A collective gasp gripped the table, but Kate didn't care. She wanted answers. *Now.*

"Why did you come to the Inn, Judith, and *why* are you leaving him? And what does it have to do with our father, because *you* wrote that article for the paper."

Amelia's eyes lit up. "The one in the lighthouse. That *was* you." Her voice dripped in poison. "'How to be a better wife' or some bull crap."

They were teaming up, and things could get ugly, but then... wasn't Judith an ugly person? Wasn't she the one who started all this? So many years ago when she bit into the apple that was Gene Carmichael and his great love of Birch Harbor and all things Nora Hannigan?

Megan spoke next, her tone even and her face calm. "Enough. Let her defend herself. She's here, isn't she? She must care, right?"

Kate took a breath and eased back in her chair, stealing a guilty glance at the girls then Michael. None of them deserved to see this. None of them needed to watch as she came utterly undone.

"I came to the Inn to make peace," Judith replied, her voice ragged. "And yes. I can tell you what Nora meant. But I can assure you it will mean precious little. Precious little."

"Anything is better than nothing," Clara murmured. "We're tired of this. We're tired of stumbling upon endless torn-out journal entries and random heirlooms that might *mean* something. My sisters have lived lifetimes under this question. They deserve anything they can get. We all do. The town does."

"The town had their answer," Judith replied. "Your mother had that right. Once they figured her for whatever it

was they figured her for, it was over. Mathers let them win."
Judith looked down, and Kate peeked at Mercy, who wilted.

"It sounds like it was never up to him to begin with. If we're going by any of this." Kate waved her hand across the notebook.

A shuddering breath caught in Judith's throat. She closed her eyes slowly then opened them, readjusting to her position there, at the end of the table. Somehow, she'd shrunk and mutated before their eyes. Gone was the stylish queen bee. In her place, a frail witch of a woman who'd just come to the realization that her cauldron had run dry. "The day your father... *left*, we had a visitor at the school."

"Which school?" Clara asked.

"St. Mary's. On the Island."

CHAPTER 30—NORA

WENDELL ACTON CASE

When I started at the church, I prayed for answers. I prayed for peace.

And while I didn't get the former, I *did* get the latter. In the form of this teacher, Judith.

Judith, you see, knew me back *then* when I was in trouble. She wasn't a good friend—I don't even recall us exchanging more than a word here or there—but she *was* around, and she surely had a sense of things.

After St. Patrick's, my next point of interest was to retrace Wendell's steps at the house on the harbor—assuming he had been there at all. I searched high and low and came up empty.

Then, I went to the marina. I asked around, but every man there reminded me *the police had already been there. Nothing new to report. No boats in or out. No Wendell.* They knew him, too. I trusted that.

He didn't need the marina to push off from Birch Harbor, though.

Likely, he left from the lighthouse, but seeing as I am forever on the outs with the Actons, I couldn't well schedule a visitation. I had to sneak over there.

With Clara in the car, I couldn't stick around or even get out of the car. Too cold and she'd be too fussy. Instead, I drove up just past the lighthouse and parked on a frosty stretch of grass. From that position, I had a view across the lake and down the shore, near to what Wendell may have seen in the lighthouse, had he stopped up there for a spell.

So, I sat and pondered. I thought about what Wendell might have been thinking about. Me. The girls. Our disagreement in how we ought to proceed.

Wendell believed that Kate and the town could handle the truth. That she'd be free of humiliation. *That it was the nineties, Nora! This sort of thing happens. Teenagers make mistakes.*

I held firm that we'd change the story, and Wendell... he didn't like that. He figured people would know, and we'd be double-humiliated—first for the teen pregnancy and second for lying and pretending a woman at my age would have another baby. That hurt, and it propelled me to hold my ground even more passionately. We could do it. We could make Clara ours, and no one would ever be the wiser.

But if I went by Wendell's line of reasoning and put myself in his shoes, then what could I see? Where would I go?

He had worried that we'd be found out... but by whom?

More religious than I, Wendell would probably pay a visit to the priest (even though we scarcely attend). I could whip back there and see if Father... *what's his name?* I can't even recall the current priest. Does Wendell know him better? Did Wendell go to him and make some sort of... confession by proxy? For Kate? To clear her sins?

Judith tells me she doesn't know.

CHAPTER 31—AMELIA

"Doesn't know what?" Amelia asked.

"Doesn't know if Wendell went to the church?" Kate added.

Clara turned the page, but before she could continue reading, Amelia reached across the table. "Wait a second. I want to address this." Then she looked at Judith. "Did Wendell come here next?"

Judith pursed her lips. "I have no idea. That's what she meant, I'm sure; it's the same thing I would have told your mother. I had no idea where he went next."

Kate let out a sigh and glanced from Amelia to Clara. "Why would Dad confess on my behalf? I don't believe that. He was too... *you know*. Just like Nora. They were both that way."

"What way?" Megan asked.

"Insular," Clara murmured.

"Insular," Judith repeated.

"What does that mean?" Mercy asked.

Amelia gave her a soft smile. "If you haven't put it together by now, we're weird. And our ancestors were weird.

And they sort of... I guess pushed their way onto the shore and never took no for an answer. You know the type?"

"Bullies?" Vivi chimed in.

Amelia thought about it for a moment, but Kate answered, "Bullies are more aggressive. Provocative. Our family kept to themselves as much as possible. Didn't share. Didn't invite."

"But that's not entirely true," Amelia pointed out. "Nora turned into quite the hostess."

"Right. And even Dad liked to have company."

"But Nora came from a long line of people who felt they had to protect the house on the harbor, and she rubbed that off onto Dad. He took it seriously, the protective thing," Megan pointed out. "I wouldn't have guessed Dad talked to *anyone* about Kate. Unless something *happened*."

As if on cue, all of them turned their heads to Judith.

Judith pointed to the journal. "Does it say she went to the Fiorillos? Is that how she discovered *me*?"

Clara shifted in her seat and looked back to the journal, flipping through pages and skimming. "I don't see anything about the Fiorillos."

"Go ahead, Clar," Kate said. "Keep reading."

Amelia reached across the table and asked, "May I?"

Clara lifted the notebook and passed it her way. "All yours. I'm getting tired of this. Long reveries with no end in sight. There's not much after that."

"Really?" Amelia asked, flipping through to see for herself. Indeed, there were just two half pages of writing left. When she looked through it herself, she was surprised to see how neat and orderly the thoughts were. This wasn't a case report like she'd have expected. Not like the scraggly chicken scratch from the useless police files. It was as though Nora had sat each night at some tidy little writing table, dabbed her quill in a perfectly round jar of ink, and set off—narrating the darkest days of her life. "*Wow,*" Amelia breathed. "This isn't any specific information. It's merely her reflections. Her musings."

"It's like her journal entries, except in a different notebook," Megan added, peering over Amelia's shoulder.

"Why not just contain it all in her journal? Why write half there and half here?" Amelia asked, skimming through the previous pages and rereading what Clara had already covered.

"That was Nora," Clara replied, frowning. "I wouldn't be surprised if we found a second diary and ten other notebooks."

"But look..." Amelia shuffled the pages like a loose deck of cards. "She left most of this thing totally blank."

"That was *Nora,*" Kate echoed Clara's words.

"Leaving stuff... unfinished?" Vivi asked.

Amelia glanced across to the three girls—Sarah, Mercy, and Vivi. How they sat patiently, allowing the others to take over and burst into this little adventure. "You three read this whole thing?" she asked, dropping the book to the table and crossing her arms.

Sarah nodded. "Twice."

"I read it three times," Mercy added.

"And you came here first? Because Nora wrote that it was a good starting place?"

Again, Sarah nodded. This time, Vivi and Mercy nodded with her. "She said when you get here, you'll know what to do and who to ask for."

"What does that mean? Does she ever specify?" Megan asked, sliding the notebook her way and cracking into it. The charm of story time had worn off, and they all turned hungry and irritable.

Sarah shook her head. "We figured it was..."

"Symbolic," Vivi said.

"*Symbolic*?" Amelia asked. "What do you mean?"

Clara pressed her hands on the table. "'What to do and who to ask for'... isn't *literal*?"

Mercy shrugged. "We thought it was, you know... *religious*."

Amelia waved her hands. "Wait a minute, wait a minute. You thought it was *figurative*, but you still came here. As if it could *result* in something?" She pushed the notebook away and stood, nearly knocking her chair back. "This is a wild goose chase." Her eyes flew to Michael, and she pointed at him. "You were wrong. We'll never find out what happened to Wendell, and we'll never find out why our mother was such a nutcase." She swallowed a sob and threw a final glance at Judith. "You said so yourself, didn't you? There's nothing you know that can change anything. We've gone back in time. We've read all there is to read, and still, here we are—orphans." Tears stung the corners of her eyes and all of a sudden, she knew why she didn't want to have a big, fat wedding with cake and attendants and a fancy dress and all the things she *should* want.

Because what if it didn't last? What if she went away on vacation one summer, and when she came back... Michael was gone?

CHAPTER 32—MEGAN

Amelia flew from the hall and into the bitter chill outside. Michael jogged after, turning only to give them a feeble look.

"Is she right?" Megan asked Judith as Kate and Clara clambered after Michael and Amelia, uselessly.

Judith winced. "I have no idea."

"You have no idea why our mother was a nutcase? Why our father left us? Or if you or these ridiculous journal entries can help?"

"All of the above?" Judith answered meekly then looked at the girls. "I haven't read what she wrote. Not like they have."

Megan turned her attention to the trio of teenagers, and her face softened.

"I mean..." Sarah started, chewing on her lower lip like she had done when she was just a kid—back when going to Grandma's house was a chore, not a quest. "I don't know." She looked helplessly to Mercy. "We knew where to go. If you read it, you can see what Grandma Nora did, and that's what we were going to do. Just... follow her trail. You know?"

Megan swallowed her anger and returned to the note-book, reading aloud for Judith to hear. Maybe having an outsider could help. Maybe even Judith Carmichael *could* help.

"Wendell Acton Case," she began, smoothing the page. *"I've decided to go against my instinct and not enlist the Fiorillos. I genuinely doubt Wendell would drag them into this mess. In fact, knowing Wendell as I do, I doubt he'd drag anyone into this mess. I have no clue where he might have gone, but I figure there is one place where I ought to go. One person I ought to visit. Logically, the police won't have suspected him. But if I don't talk to this person, then I know that the case will writhe in limbo for time and all eternity."*

There was no more on the page. As if she wanted to keep his name a secret, even though she *hadn't*. His name was in the other diary. The one they found before that led Megan and her sister to find Liesel and figure out the truth about Nora Hannigan.

She turned the page, to the next entry. It began on a different note altogether, as if Nora had skipped the good stuff. "The meeting was just what I needed to get some clar-ity. I find less time to document this while my duties to Clara and the girls remain my focus. And now, as I narrow in on the truth, I have less cause to write anything down. It's as though I'm growing free, pace by pace."

Megan frowned at the paper. "Why did she call you? What happened at the meeting?" She flipped through the pages then looked up at Judith. "None of this makes sense. She skips ahead and leaves important things out." Then Megan looked at the girls. "Does any of this make sense to you?"

They shook their heads just as Kate and Clara returned.

"We're going to take a break and grab lunch. Amelia

needs to cool off, but I think we should wait for her. Don't you?" Kate asked.

Megan shook her head. "We can fill her in. I want to know what happened between Wendell and Judith. We have her here. I want the story. Now."

She was trembling, and that was unlike Megan. Never in her life had she cared one bit about what had happened to her father. Losing him had become easy on Megan; she was the first/fastest to accept that he'd left them, and *that* was *that*. But now here they were, with *some* answers at their fingertips, and she was unwilling to drag it out any longer.

"Not without Aunt Amelia," Sarah argued. "This has been her *thing*."

"If that were true, she'd have stayed. But she's gone."

"What do you mean it's 'been her thing?'" Vivi asked.

Sarah let out a sigh. "Michael and Aunt Amelia have been studying Wendell's case since, like, May or June or something. When I lived there this summer, it was all she talked about. Then... she sort of got over it, or something. Gave up."

"And now she doesn't care?" Mercy asked meekly.

Megan glanced at Judith then Kate. "Yes," she answered the girls. "She obviously cares a lot."

"Then let's wait until she's cooled down. Grab lunch. Come back to this."

"Can you just tell us, Judith? Why Wendell came to you? Or the unfamiliar school visitor who you *think* was Wendell?"

CHAPTER 33—CLARA

Michael managed to convince Amelia to join them at the Inn. Kate asked Matt to pick up a pizza and some drinks, and in the transition, Clara had a moment to sneak off to call Jake.

He didn't answer, though.

She stood on the back deck of the Inn and squinted toward the marina, looking for him, but she didn't see Jake poking out of the office or in his boat. Gone, too, was Jake's boat—a patrol-style vessel. She didn't want there to be some sort of tragedy or emergency on the water, but she did hope that's what was keeping him out so long.

In the transition between the church and returning to the Inn, Clara had taken note of Judith's willingness to rejoin them.

Then again, if she was on the brink of a breakup, maybe she needed somewhere to lay low. Maybe she needed a place to stay, even.

Clara found her way inside to the parlor, where Matt had already arrived with the pizzas, and Megan and Sarah were setting up drinks on the coffee table.

Kate whisked away the sherry decanter and lowball glasses and set out a buffet on the bar at the far end of the room.

"Where's Amelia?" Clara asked, striding to the window and peeking out through the curtains. "Do you have any guests booked tonight, Kate?" She turned as Kate joined her, moving the curtain aside.

"No bookings. We're vacant tonight."

Clara blinked and glanced to the girls who huddled in a small circle at the bar, each with a greasy slice of pizza in one hand and a weak paper plate in the other. Nora would never have let her have pizza in the parlor. Sloppy foods could only be eaten at the kitchen bar or table. It was one of many rules that made sense to Clara. So much so, she carried them with her when they moved to the cottage, despite her mother's growing leniencies.

"There they are." Kate let the curtain fall and moved out of the parlor to the door.

Clara went for a piece of pizza herself, stealing another look at the girls, willing Mercy to tell her that she'd heard from her father—everything was fine, and he was on his way, perhaps. Or maybe he'd sent her a text saying he'd meet them at the Inn. Or maybe even that things *weren't* fine, and she ought to sit tight.

Then again, if he'd been in touch with Mercy, he'd have had a chance to get in touch with Clara. She pushed the thought out of her head and lowered herself into the sofa, next to Judith, who sat rigidly.

"Hi," Clara said softly. "I'm sorry you're stuck in all of our drama."

Judith smiled. "I'm part of it, I suppose. I invited myself in, even."

"What do you mean?"

She sucked in air and shifted on the sofa to better face Clara. "I booked a room with Kate. I knew I had something to share with you girls. But even before then... I made Megan's business *my* business."

"Shall we begin?" Kate appeared in the entryway to the parlor. Amelia stood at her side, Michael behind her. Clara's eyes flitted down Amelia's arm to where it ended, her hand in Michael's. Her gut clenched. Would she and Jake ever get to that point? Public affection, even in chaste doses?

Or had she ruined her chances?

"Yes, please." Megan flopped into the sofa, gnawing on a piece of crust.

Everyone found a place on one of the sofas or armchairs, and Michael brought two plates over for Amelia and himself. Clara stole a look at her sister, who seemed drained —emotionally and physically.

She was beginning to feel that way, too, and she wondered how the day may have panned out had it not been for the teenagers and their tear across the lake. Would they have found the truth first? Would Judith have gone home to her boat on the water, ignoring Gene Carmichael for the evening until she wandered back on land the next day, finding a new place to take cover?

It was funny thinking about Judith in that way—like some vagabond. Didn't they have a house somewhere else? On the Island or in some suburb north or south of Birch Harbor? Couldn't she escape there? And if she could, then why was she here? Why was she hanging around town like some desperate busybody? Suddenly, the question felt important. So important that Clara wanted to know the answer to *that* before she knew why Wendell went to St. Mary's.

But Clara didn't get the chance.

"I don't know if it was Wendell, but he matched the description," she began without prompting.

"Back up," Kate directed. "Can you tell us what brought our mother to call you in the first place? Can you start at the beginning?"

"Isn't it in the notebook?" Megan asked, frowning and sliding it out of her handbag.

Mercy shook her head. "No."

"So, it just skips from the church, to a phone call, to *after* the phone call, to the lighthouse, to some meeting with some mystery man?" Megan asked.

Amelia wiped her hands on a napkin and reached one out. "Here. Let me see it."

Megan passed the book her way, frustrated to within an inch of her sanity.

Amelia stared hard at the notebook, running her hand along the inside before she looked up. "Pages have been torn out."

"What?" Clara asked.

"See? Look." She flipped the notebook around and rubbed her finger over stubby, shorn pages in the centerfold. "She did it again."

CHAPTER 34—KATE

"If she tore the pages out, there had to be a reason. Either the information could get her into trouble, or she relocated it purposefully. Or it was wrong."

"Why don't we ask Judith." Megan swept a hand across the room.

Judith shrank but offered a sharp glance to Kate, nodding her head once. "Like I said. I have nothing that will change what you know."

"How can you know that?" Amelia asked. "You don't know what we know."

A giggle erupted from the loveseat where the girls sat, and Kate threw them a look.

"Gene told me about Liesel. How you all know about her."

"Is *that* what our dad visited St. Mary's for?" Amelia asked, leaning forward and staring hard at Judith.

Kate saw a flash light up her eyes. Like she'd landed on something. Something useful for once.

"Your mother called me because she got a tip that your father had come to St. Mary's. I don't know where she got the tip or how, but when she asked about a tall, thin man with tawny hair and a kind face, I knew it was the one who had stopped me that day."

Kate swallowed hard. "Go on, Judith. We're listening."

"I wouldn't have remembered the day had your mother not called me thereafter. It wasn't memorable, you see." She inhaled and drew her hands together, lacing them over her knee. "We often have looky-loo parents come by to see if a private school is right for their children—or rather, that *used* to be true. Back in the eighties and nineties, when I worked there, parents would come from Birch Harbor and Harbor Hills to see about enrollment."

"Harbor Hills?" Clara broke in.

"Yes, dear," Judith replied. "That's where we have our home now."

"Where's Harbor Hills?" Mercy made a face.

"It's a little town just south of here. Our sister city, I guess you could say," Kate explained, then nodded for Judith to go on.

Judith smiled. "It's a nice place to live." Her face hardened. "Anyway, like I said, it was common enough for a parent or two to come up to the office or wander into the Family Hall and ask about enrollment. Especially once we went mainstream."

"What do you mean 'mainstream?'" Amelia asked.

"In the late seventies, the secondary school closed. When they did that, the stigma left, too. All of a sudden, St. Mary's was a *private Catholic school on an island*, rather than a faraway school for wayward girls."

"Hm," Kate murmured, unable to hold back her interest. She'd not thought of St. Mary's as much competition for Birch Harbor United School District. But then again, Vivi had gone there. And Matt seemed to be fairly particular. Was that why he had moved to the Island to begin with?

"Okay, I think we get it. Randos used to visit the school. They don't anymore," Vivi declared, crossing her arms over her chest.

"Times have changed, Viv," Matt said. Kate could feel him park his hands behind her on the sofa back, and she wanted to slip inside them. She stole a glance at Clara, who kept her gaze away. Every time they were together—Matt and Clara—they weren't together at all. It worried Kate. Would the two ever bond? Surely, they would. Look at Vivi and Clara—they'd overcome. And if it came to forming a relationship with her very own *father*... didn't Clara *want* that?

She willed Clara to meet her gaze and smile—something, *anything*.

Clara must have felt the pull because she cleared her throat. "So, a man came by and, what? Asked if you knew Nora Hannigan?"

Judith shook her head slowly, cautiously. "Not initially."

Kate's breath caught in her chest. "What do you mean? What *did* he ask you? Or say? What did he *say*?"

Judith pressed her mouth into a line and narrowed her gaze on the middle distance, beyond the group and out through the front windows. "He wanted to know if it was true that pregnant teenagers attended St. Mary's. At first, I assumed it was for a child of his—or *worse*—but then he explained. He told me his wife had gone to the school years earlier, and he needed to know if it was a school for young mothers."

"But he *did* have a pregnant daughter," Kate protested. "He *must* have been asking for me." Her heart hurt at the thought. If it was Wendell who'd gone to St. Mary's to inquire about their programs, then it was for Kate. To... save her. To place her... To give her a life that might insulate her from the harsh world. A world that didn't exist anyway, because Nora had done such a bang-up job of convincing them that Clara was her own, and Kate was nothing more than a heartsick virgin who'd accompanied her mother on a last-ditch maternity vacation. Or something...

"He *did*?" Judith asked, her eyebrows curling into the center spot above her nose.

Kate couldn't summon the words to answer. Couldn't look at Clara... or the others.

"Yes."

The voice came from behind her.

Matt.

"Judith, Clara was *our* child. Kate had her in Arizona." His voice shook in the middle and evened out in time for him to add. "It was a secret."

Judith straightened in her seat and looked at Clara. "You? You weren't... *Nora's*?"

Clara shook her head and kept her gaze on her lap. "Apparently not."

"So, the rumors weren't true," Judith half-whispered.

Kate shook her head. "No. Nora didn't have an affair, if that's what you're referring to."

Bracing her hand against her chest, Judith protested, "I didn't know. I didn't... *know*. I didn't know *what* to think. When I spoke to her on the phone—Nora, I mean—she was just desperate to hear what Wendell was asking about. Like he'd find out her secret. I mean the *old* secret—the *baby. Her* baby." Judith shook her head then looked up sharply, focusing her eyes on Kate. "I kept it, though. That's the thing. I *kept* it."

"What do you mean you kept it?" Kate asked, setting her jaw and staring back.

"I told the man that no, we weren't a school for young mothers. Never had been. Never would be. And that's when he asked how I knew that for sure."

"What did you say?"

Judith pressed a paper-thin hand against her head. "I'm sure I told him that I knew because *I* went there, too."

"And then?" Kate pushed, fire in her chest.

"That's when he asked if I knew Nora and if she'd had a baby years earlier."

"And what did you say?" Amelia joined in as she squeezed Michael's hand.

"I told him I did know Nora, yes. And then I lied. I said she'd come to St. Mary's, yes, but she didn't come for a pregnancy. She came for a religious year. Just like me. That we went to school there for a year to study religion. That's why she'd left Birch Harbor High. She came to study the faith. Just like me."

Judith's voice shook, but something still didn't add up for Kate.

"If he asked about Nora, and you knew there was a missing man—how come you didn't connect the dots right then and there? How come you didn't realize he was Wendell?"

Judith cocked her head strangely toward Kate. "You forget... I grew up on Heirloom Island. I had been inland only occasionally. I didn't keep in touch with Nora or anyone. I was completely out of the loop then."

"Wait a minute," Clara gasped, her hands frozen against the air. "Judith—were you a *nun*?"

Nodding her head, Judith's face finally broke. "Yes. For over ten years."

Kate's voice turned hollow. "You had no idea who he was. Or what became of Nora. Or anything that was going on outside of the school."

"Right," Judith replied, her face cracking. "And that's when I had to leave. I lied. For an old friend—not even a friend. An acquaintance."

"For another woman," Amelia whispered.

Judith turned her head to Amelia, and a tiny smile pricked at her lips. "For a woman and the man in her life who needed it to be true."

"So, what happened next?" Matt asked. Kate felt the urgency in his voice. This mystery had become his, and she loved him for it.

"He seemed... relieved if I recall. Relieved but angry, too. If that makes any sense? He asked to make a call and left. Immediately. And that's what I told Nora sometime later when she called."

"But I still don't get it. If you two weren't close... why did she call *you*?"

"Well, it wasn't *me* she called. It was the school."

CHAPTER 35—AMELIA

"That clears nothing up," Amelia jumped in. "What do you mean she called the school? Did she ask for you?"

Judith pressed her hands together. "No, I'm sorry. What I mean is that I was there that day, in the front office, when the phone rang. Our secretary must have been busy or out or something, so I picked up the receiver, and it was Nora, searching for Wendell."

"I mean," Megan started, "did you make small talk? Catch up? Did she cut right to the chase?"

Judith shook her head blankly, her eyes searching her hands as they shifted to the knees of her jeans. "I don't remember." A deep divot formed between her eyebrows. "I'm sure we must have caught up a little. It would have been incredibly awkward. After so long and based on our shared history if you could call it shared. And anyway, when I read about the missing man in the newspaper, it never dawned on me that he could be the same as the one who came to the school. I was behind the times, of course, and that didn't help things. I was just... going through the motions of my life back then, you see. Teaching and serving both consumed me and turned me inside out—hollow. It's something I hate to say, because I *do* love the church. I *do*." Her eyes turned wet, and she swallowed slowly before meeting Amelia's stare. "I sort of 'came to' in the ensuing year or so. I began to reconsider how I wanted to live, and I thought about marriage and all of the things I'd sacrificed..." Her voice trailed off.

"It wasn't worth it? Taking your vows wasn't worth it?" Kate asked. Amelia caught her eye, and they shared a moment. They were hammering down toward something. It was happening. Amelia squeezed Michael's knee beside her.

"No, it *was* worth it. But... I suppose I outgrew the calling. When Nora re-entered my life, I sort of re-awakened to the world. Birch Harbor was no longer this looming threat, one entrenched in me since I was just a child. I pushed against the boundaries of my choices. My life."

"Did you and our mother reconnect?" Clara asked.

"No, no," Judith answered. "Not at all. I did, though, hear her panic, and I remembered what it was like for us as girls —being those throwaways. I didn't wish it on anyone—to suffer that all over again, and I knew she needed to hear that her secret remained safe. So, I told her it did. I told her it was safe."

"But why marry Gene, of all people?" Michael broke in, his deep voice cutting across Judith's emerging breakdown. "And why all of the... spite?"

Blanching, Judith opened her mouth then closed it. She looked down and then tried again, "I'm sorry for that. For what I've done. I just—"

"And another thing," Megan pointed out, "If you were

taught to hate Birch Harbor, then why would you pretend to care so much about it? Remember, Judith? That's why you turned me down for a permit earlier this year."

"Again, I'm sorry, Megan." Judith looked up. "I *do* care about Birch Harbor. I care about it as much as or more than I ever cared about the Island, but your mother—"

"What about her?" Amelia held her palms up and skootched to the very edge of her seat. "What about her, Judith?"

"She had *everything*!" Judith screeched, suddenly untamed. "She had everything even though she'd committed the gravest sin a woman of our generation could commit. And I put it all together, and it was hard on me, *okay*? When she called that day, I had been minding my own business, and I was happy to help a former problem child such as myself. You see, I ran away. Over and again. They figured the only way to keep me around was to increase their grip. At St. Mary's, you were never *not* supervised. Anyway, I was happy to tell Nora that I had protected her truth, kept it. And then later—*years* later when I found love —the type of love I had heard in Nora's voice and in that strange man's—the desperate love that could shake the very moorings of Birch Harbor... I thought I found what Nora Hannigan had—everything." She stopped for a breath but picked right back up. "Gene Carmichael wasn't local. There was no ancestral conflict, but he had become a local, some-how. Ingratiated himself. And he ran that school with finesse and respect, and I thought what we could have was perfect—the perfect blend of weekends on the harbor and weekdays at home. Then history bubbled back up to the surface, and I found out that Nora had *won*. That Birch Harbor wasn't mine; it was hers, and I wouldn't stand for that, you see. And Gene—"

"Oh my gosh," Amelia gasped. "Wait!"

Judith's mouth quivered into silence, and all eyes turned to Amelia. "That's it—Gene! How could we have missed it?"

"Gene? Amelia," Michael braced his hand on her waist, "You think Gene Carmichael had something to do with Wendell?"

She shook her head, "No, no. That would be way too obvious... to *us*, at least. But we haven't called him. We haven't asked *him* about that day—*those* days, rather."

"Maybe that's what Nora tore out of the journal," Sarah offered, stifling a yawn.

"Maybe," Amelia agreed, standing and pacing. "We have to get in touch with him."

"We've already been down that road, though," Clara complained. "With Nora and her pregnancy. He came clean. What more could he have to say?"

"Judith? Do you think Gene could have more to say? You're married to him." Amelia crossed her arms and paused in front of the woman.

Judith's fragile shoulders slumped forward. "I don't know. That's part of the problem."

"What problem?" Matt asked gently.

Amelia turned to him and flapped her hand back toward Judith. "They're breaking up."

"It doesn't have to do with..." Megan started, but Judith waved her off.

"No, no. It's been a long time coming. Living in a houseboat every weekend, his undying passion for the past..."

"And now we're back, and that's added to it all," Kate whispered.

"Oh, no. Not really. He was always *distracted*. And I thought I could regain his attention by becoming the thing he wanted most, you know? But I was wrong."

"No," Amelia replied. "We don't know. What did he want most?"

"Nora."

CHAPTER 36—MEGAN

"Judith, can you call him for us?" Megan asked.

"Gene?" Judith answered, pressing her hand to her chest.

"Yes." Amelia huffed. "We need to talk to him, and it might be a little easier for us to ease in with your help. And anyway, Nora's gone now. You *do* have his attention."

"Trust me," Judith answered. "It's not as easy as that."

"Did you already have him served?" Michael asked, his hands in his pockets and eyes narrowed. Megan recalled that Michael worked with Gene. This, in a way, pertained to him on a professional level.

Judith shook her head.

"See then?" Megan answered. "It'll be easy for you to pick up your phone and say *Honey, do you remember what happened back in the early nineties? That man who went missing? Winston... or Windsor or...*" Megan snapped, "*Wendell!*" She curled her lips into a smile. "See, easy."

"That is," Kate cut in, "If he doesn't know she's asking for a divorce. She doesn't need to have him served to lay the groundwork."

Judith shook her head. "He doesn't know at all."

"What does he think you've been doing this weekend, then?" Megan asked. "Staying here at the Inn, *without* him...?"

"Exactly what I'm doing—supporting a local business by sampling it." A crooked grin shaped Judith's mouth but fell quickly away. "He doesn't suspect that anyone would ever dream of leaving him, trust me."

Short laughter spread across the room, and Judith herself joined in.

Megan cocked an eyebrow. "I never would have pegged him for an arrogant fool when he was the principal at the high school. He seemed... *smarter* than that."

Judith leaned back, her fingers laced around her kneecap. "Arrogant, yes. Foolish, no. He knows beyond the shadow of a doubt that I'm at his beck and call. And even with Nora, he always assumed that the timing was wrong... not that she was in love with someone else."

"He talked to you about her?" Amelia asked.

Judith nodded. "Yes."

Megan chewed her thumbnail and sucked in a breath. "Well, if *we* called—I mean my sisters and me—how far would we get? How could we really nail down the truth?" She dropped her voice low. "*Hi Mr. Carmichael, we've cracked open the case of our missing father and suspect you know something about that...*" She raised her eyebrows to the others.

Kate stood and joined Amelia by the window. "Megan's right. If he does know something, he won't confess it to *us*."

"All right," Judith said.

"All right?" Megan echoed, flashing a glance to her sisters.

"I'll talk to him." Judith moved to her feet and smoothed

her flannel shirt down her torso. "But you should look for those missing pages. Just in case."

"In case of what?" Michael asked.

"In case he lies again."

CHAPTER 37—CLARA

Judith left, and Megan decided to usher the girls off. They didn't need to sit around the Inn, and it was clear that even they—the self-proclaimed adventurers—were turning bored. Anyway, Vivi and Mercy had a test the next day.

"Should we go study together?" Vivi asked as the trio gathered their coats and wandered toward the door.

"Sarah's going to the site to help her dad. Right, Sarah?" Megan asked.

She nodded at her mom. Megan and Brian's house project was coming along nicely, and they'd added an outbuilding for events, which Sarah was happy to help oversee. It had become her second little job after helping Amelia with the museum. If one thing was clear about Sarah, she liked to work. Liked to be busy.

"Yes, we know, Mrs. Stevenson. Vivi was referring to the unit test in Miss Hannigan's class," Mercy said.

"You can call me Clara outside of class, Merc," Clara strode to the girls to see them on their way.

"*I'm* calling her *Clara*." Vivi pursed her lips.

"Well, yeah," Mercy replied. "You're sisters."

"That's true," came a voice from behind. Clara turned to see Matt coming their way. Probably, he wanted to say goodbye to Vivi. Probably, he wanted to see her off or talk to her or *something* and *definitely* not talk to Clara.

She didn't want to talk to him, either.

Despite the growing comfort among Vivi and Clara and the other two girls, Clara still hadn't warmed to the idea that this Matt person was her father. It was awkward. He was young—her sisters' age. He was good looking. On the other hand, he was the father of one of Clara's students. And, ultimately, Matt was still a total stranger.

"Where are you girls going to study?" he asked, falling into place next to Clara. She wrapped her arms over her chest and rocked from her left foot to her right, preparing to head off into the kitchen or to the upstairs bath—Kate's bathroom.

"We could go to my place," Vivi offered.

"It sounds like your dad is staying here to help," Mercy's mouth rounded to the side of her face in the cute little thinking pose she often assumed in class.

Clara inched away, searching the area for something to do. Somewhere to be.

"I can take you back across the lake if you want."

"Or I can drop you off at Mercy's house," Sarah offered, jangling her keys like a set of gems.

"Would that be okay with Mercy's dad?" Clara couldn't help but ask, even if it wasn't entirely her business. Jake was particular about visitors. It was something she liked about him—his caution.

But Mercy just shrugged. "Why wouldn't it?"

Was there an edge in her voice? Was she implying that Clara *didn't* know him? That Clara's instinct was off?

She forced herself to shake it off. "Right, of course." Clara slid away, grabbing her purse from the end table and searching it for her phone as the girls left the Inn.

And that's when she saw it: a missed call and a voicemail from Jake. Maybe she was wrong about everything. Maybe Mercy didn't have a tone. Maybe Jake was never mad. Maybe he didn't think she was a complete weirdo for hiding the notebook with the sleepover treats only for it to become the catalyst in some grand Sunday adventure.

Pressing the phone to her ear, she slipped into the dining room and listened.

Clara, it's me. I can't meet you back at the Inn. Turns out we've got bigger issues on the lake. I'll call Mercy, too.

She pulled the phone from her ear after he said goodbye and ended the message. Clara had just one thing to cling to: at least Jake had called her first.

But then, Clara realized there was no competition. If she had any hope of making something work with Jake, she had to remember that even if Jake *had* called her first, she couldn't ever ask him to *put* her first.

That was the first rule in dating a father: the girlfriend was never the priority.

Clara slid the phone into her back pocket and returned to the parlor. Amelia and Michael sat, munching through a second round of pizza. Megan had left, apparently. Maybe to go help Brian and Sarah in the family project.

"Where's Kate?" Clara asked Amelia.

"She and Matt went onto the back deck," her sister replied between bites.

Clara swallowed and blinked. "I think I'll go home. Call

me if Judith gets in touch?" She shrugged her purse onto her shoulder and left.

The notebook was open and shared. Mercy was safely on her way home. And Jake had called and held the line—boat business repairs or whatever. No reason to hang around.

Especially if she was *still* the fifth wheel.

CHAPTER 38—KATE

"I'm worried about all of this." Kate fell onto the porch sofa, and the wind sailed out from her lips.

"I'm worried about the fact that you want to talk outside in this weather. Being on the lake this morning gave me enough of a chill to last until spring break."

"Spring break," Kate echoed. So much had changed in so little time. Not only since her mother's passing, but in the past five years—first with the boys moving out and beginning their own lives, separately from her. Then with Paul's passing. And then with history barging into the present, disrupting what might have been a new, easy normal.

What good could it possibly do for Clara to know the truth of her beginnings? Surely, it had done nothing but disrupt the poor thing's life even further.

But then—Clara seemed so hopeful. So *different*. Like she was waiting for some new beginning. First with her interest in bonding with Sarah. Then with accepting the whole Vivi debacle and coming to terms with that relationship.

And yet, there was a big piece of the puzzle missing.

"Have you and Clara spoken much?" She closed her eyes as she spoke, as if she were bracing for a storm.

Matt cleared his throat. "What do you mean?"

Kate opened her eyes and looked at him. "You know what I mean, Matt. Have you *talked* to her?"

He blew air out of his mouth and pushed a hand through his hair. "I don't know what the hell to say, Kate. Come on. I mean, after the Vivi thing, it's eggshells. You know?"

Kate nodded, allowing him that much. "Yes. That made it... harder."

"I sense her discomfort. Everyone probably does. She flinches when I walk up to her. She doesn't make eye contact. I feel like I'm dealing with a whole different world. Vivi was never *like* this."

"Clara isn't a child," Kate pointed out.

"Exactly," he argued. "Shouldn't it be easier? She's no teenager."

"Sure, but she's young, I guess. Not a child, but she's not... she hasn't *lived*. Conflict in Clara's world has been limited to tiffs with Nora and classroom management issues with people younger than herself. She's never had a serious relationship, period, and especially not with a *man*. Remember, she had *no* father. No one to set the standard for her. It's awkward." Kate pulled her legs up to her chest and wrapped her arms around her knees. "We need to try harder."

"What do you propose?" he asked, his knee bobbing up and down beside her.

Kate stared at the water. A boat cruised across their view —a patrol boat, it appeared. Jake?

He pulled up to a spot not far from the back dock. Two men onboard fiddled with the buoy bell there, throwing ropes and gesturing to each other.

"What if we have dinner. The four of us?" She threw a side look at Matt.

"You mean Clara, Jake, you, and me?"

"Yeah," Kate replied, a little smile forming on her lips. It was a simple idea, sure. But maybe simple was good right then. Especially against the backdrop of all the drama.

"Do you think the timing is right?" Matt asked, yawning and draping his arm around her shoulders.

"You mean because of Judith and the notebook?"

Matt nodded and pulled her into him.

"I think it's exactly what we need." She looked up at him and set her jaw. "We can't let all of that control our lives again. We can't, Matt. If Judith gets information from Gene, then *great*. But there's more to our lives than what happened to Wendell, you know."

Matt's hand loosened on her right shoulder. "You think he left you, don't you?"

Kate's gaze narrowed on the boat and the two men in it —working hard on some task unclear to her. "Yes," she replied. "I do."

In one sudden motion, Matt slipped from the sofa onto the ground, one knee down and the other knocking against her shoes.

"Kate." He took her hands from her knees, and her legs slipped down from the sofa.

She frowned at him. "What, Matt?"

"What are we doing here?"

"What do you mean?"

He squeezed her hands. "We're back together. We're madly in love, Kate. More than ever before. I come here and work on this place with you. You show up to my projects and give me tips. We eat dinner together. Vivi is—"

"Vivi hates me." Kate wanted to roll her eyes. Instead, she squeezed them shut again.

"She's warming up."

"And that's the problem. There's too much change. Too many big things. And now with Amelia *engaged*..." her voice trailed off.

"What's your point?"

She peered at him from a slit in her right eye.

Matt pressed his thumb into the space between her eyebrows and ran it up along her forehead, and her entire body melted forward.

"I mean I'm not ready to take this on—this Wendell stuff. I want to focus on the here and now. And all the here and now we're already tasked with. For me, that's about you and Clara finding some common ground. And me and Vivi, too, when the time is right."

"How about dinner for five then?" Matt asked, his hands framing her face.

"We're complicating things again." Kate started to shake her head, but then she reconsidered. "Wait. How about four? How about just *us*?"

"You mean the adults?" Matt asked.

"No. How about just *our* little family. Keep it simple. Right?"

"You, me, Clara, and Viv?"

"Yes," Kate answered, an easy breath leaving her chest in time for Matt to press his lips against her forehead. "Just us."

CHAPTER 39—AMELIA

"Have you heard from anyone yet?" she asked Megan over the phone Monday morning.

Amelia and Michael had their second marriage prep class the following night—they were doubling up to prepare for a winter wedding.

Amelia's initial choice was early January.

The sooner the better, she thought.

Before she had a chance to run away again.

Maybe as soon as the day after New Year's.

Michael reminded her that meant they'd be indoors, which could complicate the reception with so few local, indoor venue options. Still, living in Birch Harbor Heights meant Michael had access to the country club, and Nora would die all over again to know Amelia got married in the country club.

Although a country club wedding didn't feel fitting to Amelia. If it were warmer out, she'd opt for Megan's field. A small, intimate, family affair.

"No," Megan answered. "I talked to Kate earlier and no word yet."

Michael was at work, and without him or Sarah hanging around, Amelia was bored. "What are you doing today?"

"Well, Brian is at the site. He and Matt have basically turned into the contractors. They must be freezing, so after I get some business stuff done, I'm going to take a thermos of hot cocoa up there."

"Need some company?" Amelia asked, downing the last of her coffee and unknotting her robe.

"Sure. You can help me figure out my next event theme."

$\sim$

THEY SAT HUDDLED in a booth in Harbor Deli, Megan with a hot tea and Amelia with her third cup of coffee for the day.

"How about *Winter Woo*?" Megan asked, scribbling onto a notepad.

Amelia made a face. "Eh."

"Okay, how about *The Date Before Christmas*?"

"That's actually adorable," Amelia replied. "But what are you doing for this? And where?" She couldn't help but think of her wedding reception, but she didn't open her mouth about that.

Megan had already been chomping at the bit to sink her teeth into wedding planning. She had urged Amelia toward a summer wedding at the lighthouse, but that would never do. Firstly, Amelia didn't want to host her own wedding where she lived and worked. Sounded like a big mess. Secondly, the shoreline there was less beach and more grass, weeds, and rocks. If it were going to be a waterfront wedding —an idea which Amelia *did* favor—it'd have to be else-where. And *not* the house on the harbor, either. Amelia would want something all her own. Still, none of that mattered because she was gunning for January. Needed it to be January. Needed a date in hand to screw her courage to the sticking place.

So to speak.

And then, after that, she could get back to work at the high school, putting up a flashy, fun spring musical, and then after that, she could plan summer stock with the Players, and life would go on. Normally. Apparently.

Megan sipped her tea and flipped back a page on her scratch pad, swiveling toward Amelia. "Okay, *so*, I was thinking we rent out the Family Hall at St. Patrick's."

Amelia looked up. "What?" She frowned. "*Really?*"

Megan nodded enthusiastically, swallowing a sip of tea. "Yeah. I had the idea when we were there yesterday, actually. It's a great space, and it's separate from the actual church, basically, so it won't feel *too* religious. I mean, except for some of the things on the walls, but I don't think people will mind. I mean, Birch Harbor is super Catholic, right? And that view of the bay —my *goodness*, Amelia, have you ever noticed it? It's *insane*."

Amelia had most definitely noticed it. It was her favorite aspect of the marriage prep classes... so far.

The Family Hall was a high-ceilinged secondary building situated north of the church. The back door flung wide open to a cobblestone path that led through thick grass and into the sandy bay, shooting off east to the dock and south on a second path to the main church buildings.

Whoever had designed the whole space must have had children in mind. It was children who often took their Catechism classes in the Family Hall. Children whose *Simon Peter* plays filled the rec rooms of other churches across America. Children who, after Mass, would dash off to the Hall first, claiming dibs on donuts before reuniting with their friends in the grass and sand.

Something deep within Amelia churned.

January. January. January.

"So, before Christmas?"

"What?" Megan asked absently. She was scribbling on a fresh yellow page.

"*The Date Before Christmas*—you'll have the event before Christmas?"

Something sprung loose in Amelia. Like a leak in a dry-rot hose. Her insides had grown brittle and frail over time and finally popped a pinhole. Almost imperceptible, if not for the sister sitting directly opposite her.

"Oh, right. I think so." Megan glanced up, and her face broke open in panic. "Oh, Amelia, what's *wrong*?"

The tears began, and there was no stopping them. One after another, they rolled down her cheeks as Amelia wiped and wiped—her palms, her fingertips, the backs of her hands—none of her skin drying fast enough to keep up with the unprecedented emotion.

Amelia swallowed through a sob and reached for a napkin, blowing her nose and willing away the wash of... what? Grief? Fear? *Joy?* She shook her head. "I don't even know."

"Is it Judith? And Wendell? That whole ball of crap?" Megan was going for a lighthearted response, but Amelia could only shrug as she tried hard not to dissolve into full-blown audible wailing there, in a back booth of the deli.

"Partly," she managed, blowing her nose again and grabbing a fresh napkin to wipe her eyes. "It's everything, I think."

"Everything as in—what? The lighthouse? Is it Seasonal Affective Disorder?"

At that, Amelia snorted a laugh. "No, no. I mean, sure.

Maybe a little bit of that. But it's everything else. Plus..." she glanced up guiltily.

"Is it *Michael*?" Megan's eyes shifted to the rest of the deli before she lowered her head and her voice. "Your engagement?"

Amelia's face broke again, and she pushed the pads of her thumbs deep into the underneath of her brow bones, willing the pain to distract her from her outburst.

Megan reached across and grabbed Amelia's wrist. "Hey," she whispered, pulling her sister's hand down. "Look at me. *Amelia*, hey."

Amelia swallowed and squeezed her eyes shut hard before stilling herself and looking up. "What?"

"It's okay. You know?"

Frowning, Amelia shook her head. She didn't know. "What's okay?"

"It's okay to feel scared." Megan released Amelia's wrist and took her hands. "I was scared, too."

"And you guys almost got divorced," Amelia hissed, her mind spinning images of the hardship Megan had endured. How spiteful Megan was the last few years. How Brian didn't even come to Nora's funeral. How bad it got.

"But we didn't," Megan said calmly.

"It was awful. Marriage was hard, though. Right? Marriage *is* hard?" Amelia answered, wiping off the last of her tears.

Megan squeezed her hands then let them go, reaching for her tea and drawing it to her lips for a long sip. "Amelia, *life* is hard."

In spite of herself, Amelia laughed, effectively clearing away the last of the tears. "I don't know. I... I thought if Michael and I plan a wedding for January, that it'll come so fast that I can't leave, you know?"

"Do you love him, Am?" Megan asked earnestly.

Without hesitation, Amelia replied, "Yes. I love him *so* much. We have fun. We get along. He gives me space when I need it, and he shows up when I need him. And the reverse is true. I think I do the same for him, you know?"

"So, it's not about Michael?" Megan gave her a hard look. A meaningful one.

Amelia thought about it for a moment. "No."

"It's about marriage?"

Amelia took a sip of her coffee, letting it run over her tongue and fill her mouth before swallowing it down and nodding. "Maybe." She kept her gaze on the mug.

"You don't *have* to get married, you know," Megan pointed out.

Amelia's eyebrows pricked together. "What?"

"I mean, to be together, you don't *have* to get married."

"Aren't you a matchmaker?" Amelia asked. "Don't you believe in marriage?"

"Of course, I do. And I think you'll love being married, but sometimes we need to *hear* that, you know? Hear all of our options."

Amelia considered this. "Maybe I don't need to get married in January." She slung the thought out there like a fishing line, testing the feel of it before reeling it back in.

"Why the rush?" Megan asked.

"I'm worried I won't stay if I don't... have a deadline. You know?"

"Actually, no," Megan answered. "I don't personally know what that's like." She laughed. "But I see that's your issue. You run. You're a runner. What in the world you're running from, I don't know."

"I don't either," Amelia breathed. "But we've already set

up twice-a-week classes with Father Vann. We're loosely planning on a January date."

Megan tsked. "So, change the date. Set it for the summer. That way, venue is less of an issue. We can have it at the lighthouse, like I said and—"

Amelia blinked. "No."

"No, what?"

"If I get married, it's not going to be at the lighthouse." She gave Megan a serious look.

"Why not? It's meaningful. And beautiful, too."

Amelia started to collect her things, rummaging first in her purse to find cash. She tossed some bills onto the table and grabbed her coat. "I gotta go. I need to talk to Michael. I... Megan..." She paused, returning Megan's confused stare with an apologetic one of her own. "Do me a favor, okay?"

"What?" Megan asked. "Where are you going? What's going on?"

"Save the bay, okay?"

"What do you mean?"

"I mean host *The Date Before Christmas* somewhere else. The country club. I can ask Michael to rent the ballroom for you. Just—don't use the church for your holiday match-making thing."

"Amelia, *what are you talking about*? Why?"

Amelia pulled her coat on and hitched her purse onto her shoulder. "You're going to host something else there. Something bigger."

CHAPTER 40—CLARA

"Dinner? With you and Matt?" Clara asked. She was eating a bologna sandwich at her desk, a stack of tests piled high next to her computer, ready for grading.

Kate replied on the line, "And Vivi."

Clara flicked a glance to the door, as if the girl in question would suddenly materialize. "Vivi, too?"

"Is that okay?" Kate asked.

"Well, when?" Clara put the sandwich down and pushed it away, her appetite suddenly vanishing. She pulled the first paper on the stack into the clear space where her lunch had sat and drew a red pen from the ceramic cup at the edge of her desk. A cartoon cat cried out, "Keep your paws off my pencils!" on the side of it. Clara did have one pencil in there, but that didn't stop wannabe-comedians from pointing out to their teacher that her pens were fair game, apparently.

"Tonight?" Kate asked. "Or tomorrow, even?"

The evening before, Clara had fully expected a flirty, hours-long phone call with Jake. One where their laughter turned to whispers, and he wished her a good night and sweet dreams. One she couldn't fall asleep after.

Instead, she'd gotten another stilted text. Something about getting back in touch with her soon. That he'd had a long day on the lake and longer days ahead. It was effectively a blowoff, and indeed, Clara hadn't slept after.

That morning, however, when Mercy had bobbed into class, happy as a clam, Clara had the courage to mention something about the trouble on the water. Mercy had nodded her head vigorously. "Oh, yes. Something about the buoys," she'd said, "and how no one has checked them in, like, years." Mercy had made a face, even. "He was super cranky, Miss Hannigan."

It gave Clara some degree of comfort, but only some.

Still, because of all that, Clara's schedule was wide open. Maybe it'd even be good to book herself up a little. That way, when (and if) Jake called to ask her out again, she could be conveniently busy.

"Tonight's fine," Clara answered. "When and where?"

Kate replied. "How about The Bottle at six?"

"Kate?" Clara set her pen down and held the phone to her ear with both hands.

"Yeah, Clar?"

She thought about what to say—what to ask to prevent awkwardness. But there was nothing to say that wouldn't turn her instantly into a fourteen-year-old again. "Never mind. I... I'm looking forward to it."

CHAPTER 41—MEGAN

After Amelia whipped out of the deli, Megan collected her things, paid, and left, too. First, she swung by home, where she boiled milk, filled a Thermos, added cocoa powder, and grabbed a short stack of paper cups.

The week ahead was proving to be a slow one, and she could envision herself swinging by the worksite regularly. So long as the ground kept dry and the sky clear, the work carried on. It was fun to see her dream come to life in stages, and with Brian spending his evenings working on the app and his other software job, these were the moments Megan knew she had to steal to keep the fire they'd reignited.

"Hey, stud!" she called out, stepping from her car, her arms loaded down with the treats.

Both Brian and Matt glanced her way, and Megan smiled. "The stud on the left!" she clarified.

Matt waved her off, and Brian jogged over and swooped in to help, pecking her on the cheek as he took the Thermos and brown paper bag.

"Hot cocoa and store-bought cookies. I figured you

needed a pick-me-up." She wrapped her arms around herself and rubbed. "It's freezing today."

"This is amazing, Meg," Brian peered into the bag as they walked up to the site. "Is there enough—"

She nodded. "Should be. Depending on how hungry you all are. Or thirsty."

The worksite was limited to roofers only, plus Brian and Matt.

Brian carried the bag of cups, cookies, and the Thermos to a folding table near an exterior heat lamp.

Megan lifted an eyebrow. "Well, then. There's no scarcity of creature comforts I see."

Brian called to the men to take a break and grab a snack then turned to her. "The only real comfort here is when I see you pulling up."

She rolled her eyes but couldn't suppress a smile. "I had an idea for the Christmas event. All I have to do is connect with Michael about using the country club, and—"

"What happened to the Family Hall?" Brian replied through careful sips.

"Well," Megan started and stopped. She had an inkling about Amelia's plan, but then her sister had rushed off. Was Megan even right? Could she jinx everything if she opened her mouth to Brian? Then again, he was her husband *and* her business partner and deserved to know about the change in venue for the December event.

She changed tactics. "We came up with a great idea. It was actually *my* idea, but Amelia loved it, so I figured it was a winner. Ready for this?"

He slid his eyes to her suspiciously but nodded.

"*The Date Before Christmas.*"

Brian made a face. "As in... Christmas Eve?"

Megan's shoulders fell, and she lowered her cookie. "Crap."

"No, now hang on." He drew his fist to his mouth in a pensive pose. "It has a ring to it, I have to admit."

"Thanks." Megan's voice had turned flat.

"Let me ask you this," he said. "When are you going to host it?"

She shook her head. "I'm not sure. We need to nail that down soon. I figure we have to tread lightly around the holidays. I mean on the one hand, we have lonely people feeling even lonelier than usual. They *need* this."

"True."

"On the other hand, most of them still have family or friends to shop for... events they've already been invited to, like, as of Thanksgiving, even."

"So earlier?"

"Right," Megan answered.

"And you're thinking... what? That if it's early enough, and these people hit it off, they'll have a date *for* Christmas?"

As he said it, Megan turned sour on the idea. "Maybe it should be after, huh?"

"No, no," Brian replied. "What if we take that idea... and spin it out into something even cooler."

"Gee, thanks."

"Hear me out. Instead of *The Date Before Christmas*, what about *The Twelve Dates of Christmas*?"

Megan frowned. "If we're worried about bringing them in for just one day, how will we bring them in for twelve?"

"It's not twelve *days*, it's twelve *dates*. *Dates*," he added for emphasis.

Still, she didn't get it and shrugged before taking a bite of her cookie.

"Speed dating, Megan. You could make this one a holiday-themed speed-dating event. And if you do the math right, each client goes through twelve speed dates. Make each one like... I don't know... a minute or even five minutes. Then after, you can have a holiday mixer."

Megan's eyes lit up. "And we don't have to have it *before* Christmas when things are crazy!"

"Right. The twelve days of Christmas technically begins on December twenty-fifth, right?"

"Right," Megan agreed. "We can host any day between Christmas and..."

"New Year's." They said it at the same time, jinxing each other and laughing.

"And what holiday is even lonelier than Christmas for a single person?"

"The one where you have to kiss someone," Brian agreed, grinning.

"Could we even host it *on* New Year's Eve?" she wondered aloud.

"You could host it on New Year's Eve, sure. You could even make the mixer a full-blown New Year's Eve party," he pointed out.

"Oh, but wait." Megan's heart fell.

"What?"

"Amelia."

"What? What do you mean?"

"Her wedding. She was aiming for early January. This would be a total conflict."

"Well, it's not like she's going to have her wedding at the Family Hall at St. Patrick's." Brian chuckled and finished his cookie, wiping his hands on his jeans.

Megan's gaze fell to the grass at her feet before she looked out toward the lake. "I have to go," she said on a whisper.

"I wanted to show you the outlets," Brian started, holding a hand to the skeleton of a house. But Megan was already grabbing his shoulder and kissing him on the corner of his mouth. "Thanks, hon." She took off, striding with a purpose to her SUV.

"Megan, what is it?" he called after her.

She swiveled, walking backwards and answering, "*The Twelve Dates of Christmas*! I love it! I love *you*!"

CHAPTER 42—KATE

"Reservation for Fiorillo," Kate said to the hostess. The Bottle wasn't the fanciest restaurant on Lake Huron, but it was probably the fanciest restaurant in Birch Harbor. The dim lighting and marina theme paired with wide-open views of the lake made for an ambience perfect for a date.

Or a family meeting.

Were they a family, though? That question remained to be answered.

Matt pressed his hand into the small of her back as Kate followed Vivi and the hostess toward a booth near the window. She'd have preferred to sit outside, if it weren't for the bitter cold that would whip down the shore once the sun began its descent in the Michigan sky.

Vivi, for her part, was easy enough to coax out for dinner. For one, she liked any excuse to be on the marina or in the Village, like she was born to be out and about. Plus, Vivi and Clara had bonded in the intervening weeks. Their early-semester debacle proved a trial that served as a foundation for a budding relationship. Surprisingly.

But still, the air between Vivi and Kate hung heavy. Just as it did between Clara and Matt.

Kate hadn't practiced what she'd say, but she and Matt did brainstorm some talking points, planning on keeping things natural—a way to allow for true relationship building, rather than workshopping their emotions. The latter could only result in confrontation and pain, rather than anything productive.

"Vivi, no texting at the table," Matt mumbled.

"I'm texting *Clara*, Dad." Vivi shook her white hair off her shoulders and laid the phone facedown by her silverware, reaching for her glass of water. "She's walking in, in case you wanted to know."

Kate and Matt exchanged a look.

They had situated themselves with intention—Kate and Matt together on one side. Vivi across from Matt. Clara would sit across from Kate. That way, there was no push for eye contact, necessarily. And each person sat directly next to and across from someone he or she felt comfortable sitting next to.

"There she is." Vivi dipped her glass toward the doors, and Kate turned.

Clara was dressed fashionably in black tights and a maroon wrap dress. Kate couldn't imagine she'd worn the ensemble to work—too fancy. Almost too fancy for The Bottle, even. Was she... *trying*?

"Clara, hi." Kate stood and waved her around the table to the open seat next to Vivi.

A tight smile stretched across Clara's face as she greeted each of them by name. "Kate. Matt. Vivi. Hi, everyone."

So far, so good.

As if on cue, the waiter arrived, taking orders for drinks

and appetizers, leaving no empty moment for initial awkwardness to settle in.

Once he left, Kate sucked in a deep breath. "Clara, Vivi, tell us about your day."

"Well," they began together before glancing at each other and letting out a short laugh.

"You go first, Vivi," Clara said.

Vivi smiled and raised an eyebrow to her father. Something to tell him that things were going well, hopefully? Kate wasn't sure.

"Okay, well... math was fine. English was good." She flicked a look to Clara, smirking. "After school, we had rehearsal for the play with Amelia, and that was good, too."

"Don't you mean that was *well*?" Matt asked, tilting his head to Clara.

Kate watched with horror as Clara's eyebrows grew across the bridge of her nose in deep bewilderment.

Rushing to help him, Kate said, "I think he's making a bad grammar joke." She tried to chuckle, but Vivi and Clara just looked at each other hopelessly. "I mean... his *joke* was bad. Vivi, your grammar wasn't bad." Then Kate looked earnestly at Clara. "Was it?"

For her part, Clara's face opened, and she shook her head, smiling faintly. "No. Vivi has impeccable grammar." She nudged the younger girl with her shoulder. "One of my best students. Without question."

"Oh, really?" Vivi asked. "Even better than Mercy?"

Clara cocked her head. "You two are tied." Then she drew her finger to her lips. "But that's our secret, okay?"

Kate felt warmth rush her chest. To see the two interact so kindly wasn't only refreshing... it was validating. Like things could work out. Like maybe Vivi didn't have to love Kate—and Clara didn't have to love Matt—for them to make it. As a unit of some kind. Even with Clara grown and living separately, there was something that needed resolving between her and Kate and Matt. Was this it? This comfortable, easy dinner?

Matt raised his hands in surrender. "I was never a good student. I scraped by. I have *no* idea where Vivi gets her academic chops. Not me, that's for sure."

"Her mom, then," Clara replied.

The mood soured instantly.

Vivi cleared her throat. "My mom may have been smart, but not *that* smart."

Kate knew better than to prod. But Clara didn't. "What do you mean?"

"How smart is it to allow your daughter to live with her dad, you know?" Vivi's eyes dropped to her water glass.

The waiter interrupted again. This time with drinks.

"Thank you," Kate murmured, willing the conversation to divert away from the hard stuff.

But Matt jumped in. "*Allow* is the operative word, Viv," he said, pulling his glass of beer close. "She didn't *have* to allow you to live with me."

"She didn't fight for me," Vivi answered quietly.

"That's not true. Vivi's mom did fight for her." Matt looked at Kate, his eyes pleading as though there was something *Kate* of all people could contribute.

But the fact of the matter was, Kate knew nothing about Vivi's mom. Only her name.

Quinn.

"She fought *with* me. Not *for* me." Vivi took a sip of her iced tea then ran her tongue over her lips, narrowing her gaze on the rim of her glass.

"You have had every opportunity to spend the summers with her. Christmas break. Spring break. Vivi,"

Matt said, his voice low, "You've *chosen* not to see your mom."

"Matt," Kate interjected, a warning.

He rested his hand on hers atop the table. "You're right. A conversation for another time." Kate watched his Adam's apple bob up and down. "I'm sorry, ladies."

"I get it," Clara replied, suddenly fortified, it seemed, by the direction of the conversation. As though she had something to add.

"You do?" Vivi asked, meek as a mouse.

"Of course." Clara slid her glass away and shifted in her seat to face the younger girl. "I didn't have a good relationship with my mom." She looked at Kate. "Not this one, although we didn't have much of a relationship at all."

Kate's eyes grew wide, and she felt her face flush, but a wry grin curled up Clara's cheeks. "I'm joking. Kind of. I mean—*now* we do. Look at us, Vivi. We live in the same town. We love each other. And she didn't bother to raise me at all."

It could have been a cold thing to say. The *wrong* thing to say.

But fortunately, Vivi caught the joke and laughed, and that gave Kate permission to laugh too.

Even if she wanted to cry.

CHAPTER 43—AMELIA

When she found out Michael was in meetings all day, Amelia decided maybe it wasn't a bad thing to let her idea sit for twenty-four hours. She could sleep on it. Work with it. Then, when she had the answers, she could present them to Michael in a pat little package. Like a gift. One thing off his to-do list, which she knew was long—between attorney stuff and his time helping at Megan's property.

After all, she didn't *technically* need Michael to plan the wedding. And anyways, he'd give her carte blanche on all things wedding. The only exception being the Catholic part, which Amelia agreed as a matter of course.

Opting to work around the lighthouse the rest of Monday, she set off Tuesday morning, first thing, for St. Patrick's.

Though the air was cold, Amelia kept her window open, drinking in the shock of her great idea. The sudden comfort it offered.

All she needed was to confirm a few minor details, and

the rest would fall into place. At least... that was her hope. And she needed hope. Or an omen.

"FATHER VANN?" She peered into the front office of St. Patrick's.

"He's next door." The voice came from the deacon's wife, a plump lady of an indiscriminate age and make—somewhere north of thirty and south of a hundred. She might have ten kids. She might have none. Amelia wondered if *she* came across as elusive as that.

"Thank you," she answered, leaving the office and cutting across a grassy patch to the church. She tugged open the heavy wooden door and stepped in, anointing herself—out of habit—with holy water before opening the second set of doors, glass.

"Father Vann?" she called again into the echoing hallowed space.

"Over here!"

She stepped up to the last pew, glancing left then right.

His rear end poked out from the confessional at the far corner.

Amelia stifled a laugh. She didn't think of priests or religious clergy as having rear ends. To see it isolated like that turned her into a thirteen-year-old boy.

Smiling and shaking away the sillies, she answered, "I'm so sorry to bother you. It's, um, *me*, Amelia Hannigan?" She hated it when she identified herself like she didn't quite know who the heck she was.

After shuffling, Father Vann whipped around, wood oil and a rag in his rubber-gloved hands. "Amelia Ann," he returned.

"Need any help?" she asked, warming to him for using the name she'd given during their first meeting. She didn't know why she had introduced herself that way, but Father Vann had asked if Ann was her confirmation name, to which she replied that, no, she hadn't been confirmed. That time in the Hannigan women's lives had been too tumultuous. Father Vann hadn't blinked an eye and simply replied that he liked the name. All of it, even without the confirmation part.

"I'm just finishing up, but thanks. What can I do ya for?"

"Oh, well, I wanted to talk about our ceremony plans and the reception, too. I know that's not part of the deal, but since we're doing it all together, I figure maybe I could pick your brain? And, um, take a look at your calendar? Or I guess ask *you* to look at your calendar?" It occurred to her that she might have just asked the deacon's wife to help her, but something about Father Vann drew Amelia in, giving her a soft place to fall... just in case she did.

"My calendar, huh? Have you and Michael agreed on a date? Let me guess: New Year's Eve."

Amelia shook her head and followed him back out to the vestibule, but not before they both turned and genuflected, the movement still unfamiliar to Amelia despite her years in St. Patrick's as a girl. She'd been away for so long, the religion had become new to her.

"Oh, right. Who wants to share their anniversary with another holiday?"

Amelia didn't answer that plenty of people did. That's why Valentine's Day was one of the more popular winter wedding dates, for example. But she simply replied, "Something like that."

"Let me ask you something, Amelia Ann," he went on.

She steeled herself for a personal question. Something

spiritual. Something that would reveal her heart as impure. "All right," she answered.

"Have you got a little extra time on your hands? I know you probably don't. Not with the museum and the school play and then of course your marriage classes here." Still, he lifted a sparse eyebrow.

She swallowed. "I do have *some* spare time. During weekdays, particularly."

"Ah, that won't do. How about Sundays?"

She knew he would get down to it. The classic guilt trip. Expected.

"I, um... well, normally, I mean, there's Mass to attend, of course, but..."

He waved her off. "Listen, Amelia Ann, we need a director for this year's Nativity play. I wouldn't want to steal you from your usual duties, but if you think you might be up to it—"

"I'd love to," she answered immediately.

"Oh, you would?" His face opened wide, and Amelia smiled back.

"Of course, I would." It was perfect. And she really would love to. A way to ease back into church life in a way she was comfortable with.

"Great. That's just *great*. Tina'll be pleased, and speaking of which—let's go look at the calendar, shall we?"

"Yes," Amelia answered. "That'd be great, Father Vann. But it's not just the date I'd like to talk about."

～

THEY WERE in the front office, Father Vann with his personal calendar propped in his hand.

"And where are you having your reception, dear?" Tina,

the deacon's wife, asked, licking her thumb and flipping in her desk calendar to March.

"Well, that's what I wanted to ask about, actually."

"Oh?" Tina slid black-rimmed glasses down her nose and looked over them at Father Vann.

But just as she was about to ask her next question, something on the wall behind Tina caught Amelia's eye.

She cocked her head and pointed. "That life buoy, there."

Father Vann followed her gesture. "Yes?"

"Where did you get that?"

Father Vann frowned at it, then shook his head, lost for words. "Tina?"

"It was here when I started. I think the last deacon found it tangled up in our dock."

Amelia rounded the desk and peered more closely at the old-fashioned flotation device. Faded and mottled by time, it reminded her of the décor in The Bottle—harbor classic, as she liked to joke. But there was something about this piece that felt distinctly important.

She swallowed and stood right next to it, trying to make out the sun-bleached lettering of yore.

But try as she might, she couldn't.

She shook her head and shrugged. "Sorry. I... anyway, where were we?"

"Your reception venue, dear," Tina answered, pulling her glasses back up to her eyes and pressing a finger along the first week of March. "And you'll want to think carefully. Mighty cold here that time of year."

"Actually, I was wondering... can I reserve the Family Hall?"

CHAPTER 44—CLARA

Dinner was weird.

But not *that* weird. And it was sort of nice to see Vivi's perfect shell crack. Not that Clara *wanted* that for the girl. Not that Clara wanted that for any one of her students or anyone. Not a dysfunctional family. Not an absentee mother. And anyway, could Clara *really* relate?

No.

Because she didn't *want* to leave Nora. Not like Vivi apparently *wanted* to leave her mother. No matter how discordant their relationship at times, Clara had loved Nora as a mother, and Nora loved Clara as a daughter. Period. End of story.

And Clara suspected that Kate held that sort of affection for her, too. In her words and actions—in her soft looks and in their quiet moments, a connection was brewing, and it made things *easier* for Clara. Easier to have her sisters in town. Easier to try new things. Easier to accept her choice of staying in Birch Harbor. For the long haul.

After they picked around dessert and prodded Vivi back into a good mood, Clara found that she and Matt had something in common, too.

He was a reader.

This struck Clara as strangely funny, especially because he said he wasn't much of a student. But then he listed his favorite authors—Stephen King, Harlan Coban, James Patterson... the list went on and on. He said he grabbed a book each time he went to the store. It was how he relaxed.

Clara remarked that perhaps that's where she got a bit of her passion. Kate, however, was quick to point out that her maternal line was ripe with the written word. When Clara asked what that meant, Kate reminded her of Nora's seemingly infinite journals and diaries and notebooks.

To Clara, though, that only cemented her idea of a quirky upbringing. Nora had never once written a thing in front of Clara. And naturally, she'd never seen Nora—or even Kate, for that matter—pick up a book. Innate. All of it. A love for writing and for the written word—innate. Qualities passed down to her from some biological point of promise.

They'd ended the night on a good note, bringing Vivi back into the fold and finding common ground.

It was such a good night, in fact, that Clara hadn't bothered to charge her phone until the next morning, when she nearly overslept and scrambled to get ready for school, plugging the device in only once she was firmly into her desk chair in her classroom.

And then, when it vibrated back to life, she saw that it had worked.

Going to dinner with Kate and Matt and Vivi had *worked*.

Jake had called, left two voicemails, and sent at least five texts.

But they had nothing to do with a future date.

CHAPTER 45—KATE

B y Tuesday morning, full-on anxiety had seeped underneath Kate's skin, crawling up her arms and into her neck, settling there like the flu.

She still hadn't heard from Judith.

And to compound matters, dinner with Clara, Matt, and Vivi had been awkward in parts. Not on the whole, though. The night ended sweetly enough, with Clara and Vivi bonding over their apparent parenting issues. It didn't sit well with Kate, of course, but maybe she ought to let it go. Maybe a fresh start was still taking shape, and she still had a chance to be close with Clara... and maybe Clara and Matt still had a chance to be close with one another, too. It sure looked that way. But the discomfort welled up, pushing Kate to wonder if a second dinner—or perhaps maybe something else—would be the right move. Maybe a family day trip? Or a ferry ride? Clara seemed to have loved her date on the Birch Bell, after all.

Kate stored the brainstorming as she cleared dishes from that morning's breakfast.

Two guests felt as busy as six when it came to meals and

bed turning, and she had to get ready for the afternoon check-ins.

Equally troubling to the Clara and Matt thing was Judith's silence and absence. Where was she? What was she doing? Was she talking to Gene? Should Kate call her? Find her? Let it lie?

Her phone rang. The Inn phone—the landline.

Kate strode to it, her stomach twisting at the thought that Judith finally had news.

"Hello?"

"Kate, it's me."

She frowned. "Megan?"

"*Clara.*"

"Why are you calling the landline?" Kate asked, distracted.

"You weren't answering your cell," Clara pointed out. Kate dug in her back pocket to see a line of missed calls. She'd left it on mute—not even vibrate. And for how long? A half hour tops as she finished breakfast and bid her departing guests farewell? Who could keep up with the speed of smartphones, anyway?

She scrolled to see Clara's name four times and underneath that: Judith Carmichael.

"Oh, *shoot*. Clara, I can't talk. I've got to go—"

"Kate, no. Listen. I'm heading to the marina after school. Jake found something. Or he *thinks* he found something."

"Found *what*? What are you talking about?"

"I... I don't know. I don't really know, but he thinks it's *interesting*. Can you meet us there? Four o'clock?"

Kate chewed on her lower lip, her eyes still glued to Judith's name. "I don't think so, Clar. I have new check-ins at four. And now I've missed this call from Judith, too. Who knows what information she has?"

"Okay, well, come down to the marina when you're done. We'll be there."

"Clara, wait. What did he find?"

"Like I said, I don't know. He didn't go into detail on the phone; he just told me to meet him at the marina office at four. We're going to take a look this afternoon."

Kate's head lolled back. "Oh, *I* see."

"What?" Clara asked.

Smiling to herself, Kate shook her head. "Nothing. Nothing. But you go ahead without me. Without any of us. Okay?"

"What's that supposed to mean?" Clara asked, her tone suspicious.

"Clara, I doubt whatever Jake has to show you has anything to do with our family stuff."

A pause, then, "Well, he sure made it *seem* like it did."

Sighing, Kate answered, "Clara, what exactly did he say?"

Another pause. "He left messages last night. He said he found something interesting on the water while they were doing repairs. He said it was important. That I should see it. He asked if I was free this morning, and when I texted him back and said no, he wrote that I should come right after school."

Laughing quietly now, Kate found the moment she'd been searching for the night before.

"Clara," she began, letting out a slow breath and thinking back to the day the girl was born... the weeks after, the months and years after, and every moment since when Kate had never taken a chance to say anything useful to her own flesh and blood. Was now a moment to be useful? She hoped so. "Jake says it's important because *you* are important."

"What? Kate, *no*, you aren't hearing me—"

"Clara, I *do* hear you. I haven't been listening for a long time, but I am now. And I hope you're listening to me when I say you deserve the world. Clar, you really do. You're kind-hearted and hardworking. You're *good*. Better than any of us. I think Jake sees that. You know?"

But instead of a shudder or a weepy response, Kate was met with dead air.

Clara had hung up on her.

CHAPTER 46—MEGAN

Sarah came home abuzz on Tuesday—play rehearsal had been cancelled because of a "family emergency."

"Whose family?" Megan asked as Sarah dropped her book bag by the door and flashed her phone at Megan.

"*Our* family." Sarah smirked. "Aunt Amelia sent out a group text. *Family emergency. Rehearsal resumes tomorrow.*"

Megan narrowed her gaze suspiciously on her daughter. "Are you joking?"

"No, but I do think Aunt Amelia's *fibbing,*" Sarah shared conspiratorially.

"She can't fib," Megan reasoned. "Not with *you* on the cast. She knows you'll wonder what's up. Or freak out."

"I'm telling you: Aunt Amelia is Grade-A *preoccupied.* Mark my words, *Mother,*" Sarah snarled playfully.

Megan rolled her eyes and dragged her phone from the bar. She'd been napping when Sarah barged into the apartment, something Megan had taken up ever since the colder weather had hit. It was near impossible *not* to fall asleep cuddled up under a thick quilt with reality TV humming in the background. And with Brian busy—and happily so—both with his software tasks and the construction... Megan decided no one would mind if she drifted off between the hours of one and three.

Anyway, sharing a town with her three sisters was enough to keep Megan busy in her waking hours. That was apart from the growing matchmaking biz. Which really *was* growing. As soon as she'd plastered *The Twelve Dates of Christmas* on her business' social media accounts, she was slammed with RSVPs. And that was even *with* the dubious catch, "Location to be Announced." Speaking of which, she had a mind to call Amelia right then and there. Whatever happened with the country club? Was it a *go*? And what would Megan be hosting at the Family Hall?

She stirred her phone to life with a single vertical swipe until her vision cleared enough for her to make out a missed text.

But it wasn't from Amelia.

"Uh oh," she mumbled, yawning and rubbing sleep from her eyes.

"What's *uh oh*?" Sarah asked.

"It seems like there *is* an emergency."

"With Aunt Amelia?" Panic in Sarah's voice belied her initially blasé attitude.

Megan shook her head. "With Clara. And Jake?" It came out as a question because she didn't get it—Clara's text, that was. She read it aloud for Sarah's benefit and her own... to make sense of the words. "Come to the marina when you get this. Jake found something."

"Jake found something?" Sarah twisted her face back into something more befitting a teenage attitude. Less worrisome and more scornful.

"I don't get it, either, but I'm going to find out."

Sarah groaned. "There was nothing in Grandma Nora's notebook about the *marina*."

Megan gave her a look. "You four abandoned your little adventure a little quickly to make that assumption, don't you think?"

"Abandon it? You guys took the notebook. We figured it was out of our hands. *Literally.*"

"You read it twice," Megan pointed out. "You knew where to go next."

Sarah cocked a hand on her hip. "Yeah, well, it got too intense for us. We needed adult intervention."

"Right, well," Megan replied, "I'm guessing whatever's going on at the marina is exactly what Amelia was referring to. Are you coming?"

Sarah rose from the arm of the couch, shoving her phone into her backpack. A sly smile curled across her mouth. "Yeah. I want to see what the big deal is. Who knows? Maybe he found those missing notebook pages?"

"Maybe he found the guts to ask Clara out again," Megan led the way to the SUV.

"Maybe he found a way to get Aunt Amelia to commit to a wedding date," Sarah added, joining in the jokes.

"Maybe he found Judith Carmichael's heart." Megan laughed at that one but felt bad right after. Judith seemed to be trying. She really did.

Sarah jumped into the car. Once they were off down Harbor Ave toward the marina, she added for good measure, "Maybe he found out that we Hannigans are as crazy as everyone says."

CHAPTER 47—AMELIA

After leaving the church, Amelia couldn't wait another day—another *hour* to talk to Michael. And he was about to be family, after all, which made it a family emergency. It *was* urgent that they figure everything out, after all.

She beelined to his office, only to be held up as he shuffled from lunch meeting to afternoon meeting.

"Clients all day. It's a busy time of year," his secretary chatted pleasantly as Amelia raked her hand through her hair and slid into a chair in the waiting room.

Amelia didn't like waiting on Michael, but it was okay. She didn't do it often. And besides, he'd waited on her plenty of times. What she couldn't figure out, though, was why November was a busy time of year for a lawyer.

Settling in with a dated home improvement magazine, she thought about what might bring about the need for legal work. Did many people die in the winter? Maybe. Could be estate business, much like Nora's. Lawsuit season? Potentially. Ice was already forming in little shadowed coves on suburban sidewalks and along business fronts.

Then there was the school thing going on, and it had been heating up. Maybe that was the issue. Could there be some board member from St. Mary's in there with him now? Or a concerned parent?

She checked her phone to see if he'd gotten her text.

Nope.

Still only Clara's vague request to come to the marina on some fool's errand. Something about Jake finding something.

Amelia was so *over* all of that. Really, she was. She'd had an epiphany. She was ready to move forward.

And that's exactly why she sat in her fiancé's law office, waiting to tear into there and pull herself into his chest and feel his heart against her cheek.

"Amelia?"

She whipped her head up.

Michael stood at the edge of the hall, his eyes soft, tired crinkles spanning out from them. He smiled at his secretary and told her she could take off. He was done with appointments for the day.

Amelia stood, sucking her lips inside her teeth and lacing her fingers behind her back as she watched him stride to her, loosening his tie as he neared. "What are you doing here?"

"Didn't you get my text?" she asked, glancing past him and toward his office.

He took her cue. "No. But come on back."

Once inside his office, Michael perched on the corner of the desk.

The dark wood felt darker that time of day when the sun was on the far side of the building and sinking lower and lower.

Lamps glowed nearby, casting shadows she'd never noticed before.

Michael reached back across his desk and dragged his phone to his thigh. Amelia stood awkwardly, unsure if she ought to sit or stand or be near him or far from him. She hadn't often come to his office on a personal matter, and she didn't know how proper she ought to be. On the one hand, they were in his place of business. On the other hand, it *was* after hours... and they *were* engaged...

"You wanted to talk to me." He flashed the phone to her, and she saw he was simply reading aloud her message.

She shrugged and drew a strand of her hair between her fingers, twisting it and feeling all of four feet high and ten years old.

"Come here. You're acting weird." He opened his arms and gestured her over, and she did as he said, sliding her fingers across his palms as he tugged her close. Amelia closed her eyes briefly, sucking in a breath, smelling him and the room. Woodsmoke curled in from the cracked window—Michael liked it cold.

Amelia did, too.

"Sorry," she muttered, "I just... I have a *favor* to ask you." She pinched her eyebrows together, squeezing his hands and forcing a smile on her lips before she met his gaze.

"Anything for you," Michael murmured back, dipping his mouth to her other cheek and planting a second kiss there.

Her stomach turned to knots, and she knew her favor would disappoint him. Still, she pressed her hands on his chest and stared hard at him. "Michael? Can Megan and Brian use the country club for a matchmaking Christmas party?"

He blinked. "I don't know. When? And... *why*?"

"Because..." Amelia swallowed before she went on, "She was going to use a different venue for it, but I asked her not to."

He shook his head slowly. "Okay. You've lost me."

"I *think*—no. I *know* I'd like to have our reception at St. Patrick's."

"We're having the *ceremony* at St. Patrick's, Amelia." His voice was quiet. Calm. But something simmered beneath it.

She nibbled her bottom lip but pushed on. "Michael, I really love the Family Hall."

"The Family Hall? At St. *Patrick's*?" he chuckled, but his quick glance off and away, and the loosening in his grip revealed his churning unease.

She squeezed his hands tighter. "Yes. The Family Hall at St. Patrick's. It's a bigger space... the view is brilliant, Michael." Her eyes lit up as she reimagined it now. "It feels right to me. I can't explain it. It just... it's calling me. Pulling me, I guess."

"Well, it would eliminate the problem of freezing our tails off, I guess." He smiled and returned her grip with another squeeze. "We'll have our wedding wherever in the world you want to. Okay?" Michael tugged her toward him and kissed her in the perfect center of her forehead.

Amelia melted into his chest, pressing her cheek to his heart and listening to it. Trying to discern if it was true. If she could predict if he'd leave her. If having the reception in the Family Hall would help make things feel as perfect as she needed them to.

Or if Michael would be just another Wendell Acton.

CHAPTER 48—CLARA

Clara stood on the edge of the dock, her toes hanging over precariously like she wanted to jump. She wanted to feel the shock of frigid water. She wanted to know that she was alive and not dreaming this. She wanted to know that *everything* was cold.

Not just Jake.

Despite his chilly behavior in the preceding days, Jake had summoned her here. Pulled her here, to be with him. To meet *him* at the marina—at the lake—and to show her what, exactly, he'd spent the last few days working on. What he'd *found*.

On the one hand, she silently wished he'd ferry her out to the Island, and they'd tuck away inside of a little café she didn't know about. Just like Kate had predicted.

On the other hand, she wanted him to reveal something substantive. Something that would make a dent in her world—an impact. The truth about her sisters' father. The truth about *something*.

"Clara?"

She whipped around.

Jake strode down, crossing from the cobble path onto the dock, closing on her pace by pace. She looked past him to the office. Had he been in there? Seen her walk by, searching for him?

"Sorry I'm late. Had to coordinate pick-up for Mercy." He hooked his thumb back up to the marina parking lot.

She squinted. "Didn't she have play practice?"

"No. Rehearsal was cancelled, but she's getting a ride with Paige. I wish I knew that before I made it halfway to school." He shook his head and stopped at a piling. Just two feet away from her. Close enough to fall into a hug. Close enough to close the gap and kiss.

Far enough to do neither.

She pressed her mouth into a line. "What did you call me out here for?" It was the obvious question. Simple, too. Safe.

"It's just that... I don't know if this means anything, but, well—" he faltered, shoving his hands into his pockets and looking out across the water. He wore no sunglasses. He was dressed in his work clothes—khaki slacks, a white long-sleeved cotton polo. An orange vest zipped over it.

"Are you still on the clock?" she asked, filling the awkward moment.

He glanced down at himself. "Oh, right. This." He pinched the emblem on the vest. *Birch Harbor Marina.* "No, I'm not."

Clara shielded her eyes from the sun that set behind him. "But you found something? On the lake? Or... *in* it?"

Jake's expression changed. Surprise colored his cheeks and lifted his eyebrows. "No. Um." He pushed his hand through his hair and let out a short laugh. "No, that's not what I meant."

Clara took a step backward, and her heel bowed low off

the edge. Her hands flew up in front of her as she tried to regain balance, but the step had caught her too far off guard, and she was sailing in reverse, away from Jake.

He lunged forward, gripping her flailing wrist with one hand, jerking her onto the dock, and swinging his other arm around her waist to right her. Comfort her. Hold her.

"Whoa there," he murmured, his hand still pressing her into him. "Are you okay?"

"Fine," she answered, mentally reviewing what had just happened. "I'm fine. I think."

"That was a close one. Come here, let's stand away from the water." He gently guided her to the center of the dock.

Clara cleared her mind from the almost fall and Jake's heroic reaction. "Thank you," she said, taking a deep breath as he dropped his hand from her back and resumed the two-foot distance. She looked up toward the parking lot and then over to the house on the harbor.

Maybe Kate *did* know what she was talking about. Was the "discovery" Jake had alluded to something intangible? A decoy? An emotional trap that Clara *wanted* to fall into?

Maybe.

But then...

"Um, about what you... *found*..." she started, chewing her lower lip and fidgeting her fingers.

His eyes passed down to her hands and then back up to her face. "Right, yes. So—" His chest rose and fell, and he cleared his throat, but Clara threw up a hand.

"I'm sorry, Jake—I figured you had actually *found* something, and—"

"Clara, I want to apologize. I've been... aloof. I've been weird, a bit, too."

"Weird?" She frowned. "What do you mean?"

His jaw locked into place. "When you told me about the

notebook, I got a little... scared." He shook his head. "That's a lie."

Clara's heart sank, and she stopped chewing her lip, running her tongue over it and crossing her arms. "What's a lie?"

"Clara, I've been scared this whole time, okay?"

She let her gaze search left and right, perfunctorily, as she thought of a response. Clearly, he was breaking up with her. Clearly, Kate *was* wrong. And Clara was, too. Megan couldn't arrive soon enough.

"I get it." She uncrossed and re-crossed her arms, this time for comfort against the biting chill. "It's really okay, Jake."

"No, you don't understand." His eyes flashed, and he inched toward her. "Clara, I've been scared since my—since Mercy's mother died."

"Your wife," Clara offered sincerely. "You can say it. Your wife. She was your wife."

A small smile formed across his mouth. "My wife."

Clara smiled, too. A sad one, too.

He blew out a breath and inched closer again, shoving his hands back into his pockets. "And then there's Mercy," he added.

Clara nodded. She had known Mercy's existence could be a complication, of course. Clara herself had often been guilty of judging parents who brought their dates around their kids. It always seemed... problematic to her. But there she was, dating a kid's parent. Her favorite kid's, too. How she had thought it would go well was beyond her. "I get it. You need to protect her. And her memory of her mother. I get it, Jake." And Clara did.

"That's not quite what I mean." He lifted a hand and

pushed it through his hair again, leaving it hooked on the back of his neck as he stared hard at Clara.

Despite the inevitable bomb he was about to drop, she felt... good under his gaze. Attractive, maybe. Important. *Seen*. Was that how he saw her? Was that the reflection in his stare? Any one of those things? All of them?

"What *do* you mean, then?" Clara murmured back.

"Mercy *loves* you. When she talks about you—when she *looks* at you—it's like she's looking at... somebody she's close to, I guess."

"And that's bad?"

"No, but it has me *reeling*, Clara. I can't tell what it is—are you like a sister to her? And if you are... then doesn't that make me... a monster? Exactly the thing that I almost became back in September?"

Clara frowned and shook her head. "No, Jake. *What*? I'm nearly thirty years old. I'm an adult. I have a career. A house. I'm not a *child*, Jake." Petulant. That's how she sounded. Petulant. Exactly like the character she drew herself to be when she planted that stupid, useless notebook which inadvertently sent the girls off on a stupid, useless goose chase.

"I know all of that," Jake hissed back, moving another inch closer and dropping his hand back into his pocket and his chin to his chest. "I *know* that, Clara." He squeezed his eyes shut then looked past her. "Can we—can I take you out? On the lake? I just feel... *better* on the water."

Clara twisted to see his boat rocking in its berth yards behind them then turned back and searched the parking lot again.

"Okay," she said. "But my sister is on her way."

"Which one?"

"Megan. I... I thought when you said you *found* something, that you actually *found* something."

Jake smiled wryly. "What would I *find* here?" He lifted his arms as if to indicate the all-but-dead marina. The empty dock. The inky, cold water. "Do you mean about your dad?"

Clara shrugged. "I don't know. I guess... I guess since you kept talking about the busted buoys—"

"Clara!"

"Darn it," Clara whispered, her eyes flying to the source of the cry.

Jake turned, and they both stared as Megan and Sarah made their way down past the marina office and toward the dock, each tucked inside layers of flannel.

"Hi, ladies," Jake smiled tightly. "How are you?"

Sarah murmured a lukewarm response.

"We're curious," Megan answered pointedly.

Clara glowered at her sister and niece, lifting her hand to her throat and slicing across it.

"What's going—" Sarah started, but Megan cut her off. She must have assumed Clara had said nothing about expecting her.

"Oh, we were... um... *curious* about what you two were doing here. But we've got a walk to take." She twisted to Sarah. "Right? We were just about to take a walk through Birch Village. Hm, Sarah?" Her voice sharpened to a point on her daughter's name. Clara laced her fingers into a grateful ball and positioned it beneath her chin, mouthing, "*Thank you.*"

But Sarah wasn't as seasoned in misunderstandings between women and the men they loved. "I thought Mr. Hennings—"

Jake, unsure how to navigate the waters of the confusion himself, lifted his eyebrows, and—to Clara's surprise—played along. "Found something. Yes. We did find something. Clara and I did. Last time I took her on the water. Has to do with the buoys. I wanted to revisit it, actually. We'll go check it out, and then we'll report back. If you'll be in the area?"

He didn't need to do that. Megan had taken the hint, and he already knew she'd been summoned. But still, it was clear he wasn't entirely comfortable revealing the truth about why he had lured Clara to the marina.

Clara, for her part, wasn't entirely comfortable with the truth, either.

Still, once her sister and niece bid an awkward farewell and backed away slowly, Clara turned to him. "Did you really want to show me the buoy?"

He shrugged and grinned. "No. But I did want to take you for a ride on the lake."

"I heard ice was forming," she cautioned.

"Only in the coves. And besides, I'd love to show you what we did—what we *do*. On the lake. Kind of like a tour of my job. It'll... give us a chance to talk, anyway. Right?"

Clara wasn't dense. Really she wasn't. But still, she couldn't quite grasp the extent of their meeting purpose. "Talk about what?"

Jake pulled a ring of keys from his pocket, grabbed her hand, and pulled her gently down the dock. "Us," he replied.

CHAPTER 49—KATE

Kate had called Judith as soon as she got off the phone with Clara, but there was no answer.

Dedicating the rest of the day to a deep clean of the bathrooms, she tried to put Judith and all things Wendell and Gene and Nora *out* of her mind.

But it didn't stop her from checking her phone every ten minutes.

Still, by four in the afternoon, there was no returned call or text.

With her new guests set to walk in the door at any moment, Kate couldn't meet Clara. Matt was at the build site with Brian all day. Vivi and Sarah had play rehearsal with Amelia.

She was alone for the moment.

Bored and antsy, she texted Megan.

Megan answered quickly. Too quickly. *Walking the Village with Sarah. Clara and Jake are going out on the lake.*

Sarah's not at school? Rehearsal? Kate tapped out the message and hit send.

Megan answered again right away. *Amelia had an emergency.*

Kate narrowed her gaze on the screen, writing back frantically. *What emergency???*

I thought it was Jake's secret discovery... turns out his discovery had more to do with a romantic rendezvous and less to do with an actual discovery...

At that, Kate smiled. She had had a feeling something was up. After all, what could Jake possibly find in the water or near it that had to do with *Clara Hannigan*, of all people? Nothing, that's what.

But then, what was Amelia's emergency? Megan clearly had her wires crossed, but still. Kate left the text thread and swiped a call through to Amelia. It rang four times before the doorbell chimed.

Clicking off as soon as Amelia's voicemail chimed to life, Kate strode to answer the door, ushering in none other than Judith Carmichael, herself. In the flesh.

Kate looked past her to a frosty front yard and the empty street beyond.

"Are you my four o'clock check-in?" she asked, bewildered.

Judith cocked her head. "Hm?"

"I have one reservation checking in at four. A party of two. Did you book with me for tonight?" Kate ushered her in. "You and Gene, perhaps?" She flashed one more glance outside before closing the door behind them.

"No, no. I came by because you didn't answer your phone this morning."

Kate pressed the heel of her hand to her head. "Right— and I'm very sorry about that." She turned and propped her hands on her hips. "But I tried to get back in touch with you immediately. As soon as I got your message."

Judith waved a hand. "Never mind that, I have *news*. I talked to him." Her eyes were fiery, and her voice rattled so that Kate could forgive her for the drop-in. It was something Nora would do, too. If you didn't answer her call, she'd ignore yours but show up hours later. She'd done that to Kate at her house out in suburbia, even.

"Come." Kate gestured to the parlor. "Sit, please."

Once Judith perched herself on the edge of the rocking chair, Kate tucked the curtain behind its hook and anchored herself at the window. She pointed outside. "Like I said, I'm expecting guests. Hope you don't mind."

"No, no. Not at all." Judith ran her hands down the thighs of her jeans as she stared out the window, too. Though her stare was hollow. Shaken.

Before she had much of a chance to crack into Judith's revelation, Kate spied a portly couple picking their way along the sidewalk, the woman clinging to the man's elbow and the man moving slowly, with precision and diligence.

Kate could see Matt being like that one day. With Kate on his arm as he led her carefully in—in *where*? To what? What *was* going to become of Kate and Matt? Would they just exist as middle-aged boyfriend and girlfriend for eternity?

A common-law marriage didn't happen if they didn't *actually* share a home—a life.

She thought back to the dinner—the lack of resolution that she felt she needed. The ongoing weirdness with Vivi. With Matt, too. Like something... or *someone* was missing from the equation. Though for the life of her, Kate couldn't pin down who? Another man to balance the estrogen? No, surely not. It was like a ghost hung around whenever Vivi and Kate got together. And the same had been true with

Clara and Matt, although they had hit it off better than Vivi and Kate had.

"Judith, let me just get these folks checked in. I'll be right back. Hold that thought. Please."

She left and opened the front door, inviting the two new faces to her front desk where Kate did what she did best: sell the small-town experience that *was* Birch Harbor. And sell it, Kate could. After all, she was *the* lone bed-and-breakfast owner.

Once the couple was situated upstairs, changing from their traveling clothes so they could make their way to the Village for dinner, Kate swooped back down to Judith.

"So sorry."

"Really, it's fine." Judith had remained in the exact same spot where Kate had left her. She wasn't browsing her phone idly. She wasn't pacing the room, studying the Hannigan family portraits like she had on a previous visit.

She just sat there, staring out the window onto Harbor Avenue as thin, scratchy branches of birch trees swung in and out of view.

Kate lowered onto the loveseat across from Judith, sinking back slowly and wondering if she ought to call her sisters. Was the information significant? Would it demand a family meeting? Would that scare Judith off?

Instead of asking or reaching for her phone, she began by offering the only thing she could—something that might help, regardless of what Judith had to share or not.

"Judith?" she asked, swallowing.

Judith's gaze pulled off the window and found Kate. She smiled. A sad smile.

"Would you like to stay here tonight?"

CHAPTER 50—AMELIA

She didn't technically have an *emergency,* per se, but Amelia *did* have several reasons to cancel rehearsal and stay home.

One, Michael had called, and he had news.

On the phone, he had asked if she could meet at the lighthouse or whether he ought to swing by the auditorium.

Two, Amelia was wiped out—emotionally and physically. With so much on her plate—Thanksgiving... the school play... the Nativity play... the wedding—she needed an afternoon *off.* She needed to play hooky.

Three, they had marriage prep class that very night.

And so, instead of scooting a dawdling couple off (*In town for the weekend! We just love small towns,* they kept repeating), she let them linger and give her a *fourth* reason to cancel rehearsal. So, she invited Michael to join her for a hot cocoa in front of the fire before sending a group text that rehearsal was cancelled for the day. It would resume the next afternoon. They deserved it, anyway. The kids were harder workers than she'd expected. Learning their lines in no time and showing up every single day to practice, practice, practice.

Michael readily agreed to come over, arriving with a cheesy schoolboy grin and a bag of marshmallows. "Sustenance," he declared at the door.

The little couple had made their way into their car, and Amelia waved them off, inviting them back anytime.

"Shouldn't you give them a card or a coupon or something?" Michael checked when she didn't move from the deck.

She pawed him playfully. "Don't you think I *started* with that? And anyway, they've been here for two hours somehow. I don't see what more they could discover if they ever came back."

"History is always in the making, you know." Michael dipped his mouth to hers and kissed her sweetly.

"Mmm," she agreed as she plucked the bag from his hand and let him in, pointing to a motley stack of firewood she'd hauled in from the back deck. "Can you start me a fire? Pretty please with a cherry on top?"

Michael shook his head and slapped his hands together. "You need to get the hang of this. It's *freezing* in here. Either that or turn the furnace on."

"I *like* it cold," she reminded him. "You do, too. I thought."

"Cold, yes. *Freezing*, no." He set about stacking three logs at odd angles, slipping a fire starter beneath the grate and lighting it in one quick motion. The whole thing roared to life within moments, and Amelia's eyes glassed over as she hugged the package of marshmallows against her chest.

"Hot cocoa, right?" Michael moved to the kitchen and expertly pulled two mugs from the cabinet before pouring milk into the kettle and setting it to boil.

Amelia followed him and tore the bag open, popping a few marshmallows into her mouth then offering it to him. He accepted, scooping his hand in and popping a glob of the stuff into his mouth before he reached across her and found the cocoa powder, sitting in wait just in front of a tub of oatmeal. "Predictable," he joked.

"Speaking of predictable," Amelia answered, "What's the plan when we're married?"

It came out of nowhere, and she knew good and well that Michael would have no idea what she meant *at all*. But they needed to have the conversation. One they should have had by now. Especially with their next marriage prep class taking place in just two hours.

"The plan when we're married?" he repeated, frowning deeply. "The plan for... what?"

"Everything," Amelia mumbled, leaning against the cabinet and taking another handful of marshmallows.

"Everything?" he repeated her again.

She gave him a look, and he held his hands up in surrender. "Okay, okay. I'll try to read your mind if that's what you want. Let's see." He tapped a finger on his mouth, and she let herself smile at his silliness. "Your father's case feels like a hot topic again."

Amelia winced. That was exactly *opposite* of what she wanted to talk about at the moment. Still, she couldn't help but be curious what he had up his sleeve lately. Michael seemed dead set on solving the thing, as if it had become a point of pride more than anything else.

"Well," he went on, "I dug up some more on Mathers after we got the scoop from the notebook. The missing girl thing checked out. She's fine, by the way. Lives in Harbor Hills now, in fact. She's a little younger than Megan, I think."

"That's... comforting, I guess."

He shrugged. "It's good to know that there was a legitimate reason for the detective's distraction, but I mean come on? Why did he give up? Was he paid off? And if so—by whom?"

Amelia gave him a look. "Do you have a guess?"

He pursed his lips. "You already know I do."

Amelia rolled her eyes. "Gene Carmichael," she said, mimicking Michael's baritone voice.

"All I'm saying is, he had *motive*."

At that, Amelia plopped the bag of marshmallows on the counter and rubbed her fingertips on a nearby dishtowel. "Too obvious. And he was, like, our *principal*. You think he was up to no good?"

"I definitely think he was up to no good. Especially when it came to your mom."

"This was the 1990s, Michael. Not the 1900s. You can't get away with carrying out a grudge in the modern age. People know about it. They *see*."

"You girls didn't, though," he pointed out as the kettle whistled.

Amelia sighed. "Regardless of how much he was in love with Nora, I don't see him engaging in, what? Foul play? That would be—*sensational*." Her stomach churned at the thought of her father getting hurt. It couldn't be true. If it were true, and she and her sisters and mother had never considered that—then what did that make them? Evil? Bad women?

No, no. Amelia needed Wendell Acton to be a deadbeat.

She flicked her eyes to Michael. Or did she?

"What news did you have, by the way?" she asked, effectively ending their line of inquiry.

"Do you want to start with *that*, or did you want to start

with my answers to what we're going to do once we're married?"

She batted him, but he grabbed her hand and pulled her in. "My answer," he went on, "is whatever you *want* to do." Then he winked and pressed his mouth onto hers.

Amelia loved moments like these. Would it all change? Once they were wedded? Would things taper off awkwardly? Painfully?

"Where are we going to live?" she asked.

"We've talked about this, Am," Michael answered, finally growing tired of just how effective she was at beating a dead horse.

"Wherever I want," she murmured. "But I don't know where I want to live. Maybe I want to stay here."

"Then we live here."

"What about your house, though?"

Michael sighed. "We don't have to make any hasty decisions one way or another. If we live here, I'll keep the house until we choose to rent it out or list it or whatever."

"But it was your family's house. Your parents."

"So is this one. Yours."

Amelia glanced around the place and drummed her fingers on the countertop. "True, but we can't have *kids* here."

At that, Michael stopped mid-cocoa stir. "There's a new one."

Amelia flushed. "I know. I know—we're... *older*."

"No, no. I'm not... judging you." The words came out quietly. Stilted. But his face was soft, earnest.

Amelia raked her fingers through her hair. "Maybe we adopt? Who knows? When Judith was talking about orphans and the church—"

"I agree," Michael answered. "It about killed me. It always kills me. The thought of parentless kids."

Amelia herself didn't grow up parentless. But she'd become half-parentless by high school, and that was enough pain to show her just how hard life *could* be. She couldn't imagine what a true orphan went through. "I like that idea, Michael."

"And you think the Harbor Heights house is better for kids?"

She frowned. "Maybe. I don't know."

"Hey now." Michael handed her a steaming mug, "There's no rush. We can figure things out as we go. Right?"

"Right." Amelia let out a long breath. "*Right.*"

"And as for my news," he continued, sipping his cocoa until a brown mustache formed on his upper lip. Amelia wiped it with her thumb.

"Yes, your news?"

"Megan can use the country club. I got permission to let her borrow the ballroom. As a friend of the club." He winked. "But there's one condition."

"What's that?" Amelia asked, bracing for something snooty or impossible.

"You let her plan the wedding."

Amelia's stomach clenched. "If Megan plans the wedding..." she started.

"Then you can focus on other things." Michael extracted her mug and looped his arms around her waist, spinning her in a slow circle like there was music in the background. But there wasn't. And she didn't want her sister to go over-board. Yes, a little help would be nice. Yes, she wanted Megan to decorate, sure. No, not plan a full-blown wedding.

"Focus on what other things?" Amelia asked.

"Whatever you *want*," Michael whispered in her ear.

"Whatever in the world makes my girl happy—that's what I want you to focus on."

A single tear welled in the corner of her eye. She knew he meant well. She *knew* he was trying. But wasn't her own wedding *exactly* what a happy bride ought to be focusing on?

And if she wasn't... then what in the world *was* she focusing on?

In the distance, her phone chimed. Once. Twice. Three times.

"You gonna get that?" Michael had released her to drink her cocoa, and he was doing the same, now distracted by an errant newspaper opened to the local news.

Amelia tugged the comics loose from the back and sank into her chair. "No. I'm taking the night off."

"Off what? Or should I say... whom?"

"Everything and everyone except *you*, my love." As Amelia said it, her eyes flitted over to the corner comics— those single-bubble ones with fewer words, no real story, just a one line jab to the gut.

"Am I *off* too? Or should we respond to this?" Michael asked, flashing his phone screen to her.

Amelia frowned at it, making sense of seeing her own sister's name on someone else's device. And then making sense of the message from Kate. *Judith is at the Inn. She talked to Gene. Get here NOW.*

CHAPTER 51—MEGAN

Walking the lake with Sarah felt good. They didn't get mother-daughter time as often anymore, and soon enough, Sarah would be gone for good.

Well, not *good* good... but she'd be gone. Off to college. Then her own life.

"Do you think you'll ever come back to Birch Harbor?" she asked, unable to keep the question in.

"What are you talking about, Mom?" Sarah bent down and collected a smooth pebble, chucking it far into the lake.

"I mean after you're grown up. When you have your own family and all that."

Sarah gave her a sidelong look. "I have no idea. Maybe. Maybe I won't even leave to begin with."

Megan stopped. "What?"

"Mom, your business is going *so* well. And Aunt Amelia needs my help at the lighthouse. I mean... what if I take a gap year?"

"Sarah," Megan answered, shaking her head and walking again, "a gap year is if you want to travel or something. Save money. You're starting college next fall. It's already in motion."

Megan steeled herself for a rebuttal, but when Sarah remained quiet, she wrapped an arm around her shoulders and tugged her in, forcing them to walk awkwardly in the sand. "You can always come back. You won't leave until August, anyway. There's plenty of time to be here." Megan didn't consider the fact that Sarah definitely *wanted* to stay in town.

"Yeah, I know, Mom. I just—I don't know what I'm going to study. I don't know what I'm going to do with my life. And my friends will be here still."

Megan sucked in a breath. "Vivi and Mercy are a lot younger, Sarah."

"I *know*, Mom. But Aunt Amelia, too. And Clara and I are bonding. It'd suck to leave my progress."

Megan dropped her arm from Sarah's shoulders and collected her hand, squeezing it. She thought about her advice to Amelia. The *out* about not getting married at all. "Well, if you want—you could start out in the dorm and see how it goes. Right? Give it a semester. You don't have to *stay*. Just try it."

"And then what?" Sarah asked, her lower lip tucked beneath her top teeth as she looked at her mom.

"And then you come home," Megan answered. "And you commute. It's less than an hour. You could do that if you had to. Right?"

Sarah nodded slowly. "Yeah, okay. I mean... as long as you and Dad *want* me back."

"Are you kidding me? What'll *happen* is we'll end up *begging* you to come home. You won't want to. Mark my words."

"Yeah, well, what if I *do* come home, and you two have gone and split up again?"

Megan laughed. A hearty belly laugh that erupted from her like a reflex. The question *was* laughable, too. That she and Brian had ever gotten so bad. Truly laughable.

In the time since the "Divorce that Wasn't," as her sisters had taken to calling it, Megan and Brian had found their groove. Their space and their connection—when to be together, when not to. Each had passion projects. But both had common goals, too. It was as though things had settled in just so. Megan couldn't help but wonder what the next phase—the empty nest—had in store for her and her husband. Maybe that would be the welcome silver lining in Sarah's departure the following year. Megan thought so, anyway.

"Sweetheart, I have a feeling that when you *do* come home, you'll find that we're more obnoxiously in love than ever." She winked at Sarah who pretended to gag.

"Okay, *okay*, forget I mentioned it!" She laughed, too, and Megan slowed, peering up into Birch Village.

Megan pointed. "Pizza? You've gotta be starving."

"Sure," Sarah agreed. "You can bore me with your latest matchmaking drama."

They cut up the wooden steps. "No drama here. Just planning the holiday event."

"Okay, then I'll bore you with *my* drama."

"You have drama?" Megan asked, rolling her eyes playfully and dragging herself onto the back deck of the pizzeria, where a shiver slid down her spine as a wall of wind shocked them.

"Not me, I guess. But the girls do."

"The girls *always* do," Megan answered, thinking about

precocious Vivi and innocent Mercy. Such an oddball couple of friends. "So, tell me. What's their latest?"

"Oh, you know. They just can't keep their noses out of the Wendell stuff."

When Sarah called her grandfather *Wendell*, it landed like a soft punch to the gut. A reminder that Sarah had never known him—a grandfather or anything else, for that matter. A feeling of sadness curled her lips inside her teeth.

"What do you mean?"

They tucked into a booth inside the restaurant, Megan plucking a menu from between the parmesan cheese shaker and a crystal candleholder.

Sarah fiddled with her phone, peeling the case back and letting it slide back into place, over and again. "I guess they dug around in the basement out in that old hunting cabin where Mercy lives."

Megan's heart dropped. "What?"

"Yeah." Sarah shrugged then looked up, shrinking back as she took in her mother's reaction, no doubt. "They already gave it to Matt."

"Gave *what* to Matt?" Heat crawled up Megan's neck. She'd figured the whole Wendell thing was done. Buried. Nothing came from the notebook. Nothing came from the girls' boat ride across the water or from Judith, the small-town gossip. *Nothing.*

Sarah flipped her phone face down and laced her fingers on top of it, fidgeting her thumbs. "I thought you *knew*," she said. "Matt told Vivi he'd give it to Kate."

"What *is* it, Sarah?"

"The missing journal entries, *Mom*. They found the *missing pages*. In some... *file* that Mercy's granddad had in a cabinet down there. A police file or something. They were in there."

Megan grabbed her daughter's wrist, the menu falling away onto the vinyl booth bench. "Sarah, *what* did the pages say? What did Nora *say*?"

CHAPTER 52—CLARA

They drifted again on the far side of the Island, and it felt a lot like their last date out there—on the lake. Colder. Both in terms of the weather and their moods. But a thaw was settling in.

Once they neared the area Jake had shown her before—his secret dream plot—she found the nerve to broach the topic, since he still hadn't said much.

"Us," she called across to him from the bench.

He whipped his head back, killing the engine and letting the boat stall.

"What's that?"

Jake drew his sunglasses down—he didn't need them anymore. The sun threw a warm red glow across the lake, and his back was turned on it anyway.

"You said we'd talk about 'us?'"

Jake moved to the bench, lowering himself next to her, his face somber. "Yes. I did want to talk about that." He lifted his eyes to Clara. "I really like you, Clara. There's no question about that."

"I like you, too, Jake." Was there a question about *that*?

Had Clara mentally moved on? Emotionally moved on? Or had her guard formed only when he cooled toward her?

"And the fact that Mercy likes you—"

"It's awkward," Clara offered.

But he shook his head. "No. No, it's not awkward. It's *good*. Does it make me nervous?" He tossed his head back and shook it. "Hell, yes. What happens if things..."

"If things don't go well?" Clara swallowed a growing lump in her throat. She wasn't okay with being held hostage on a breakup voyage. She eyed the Island. Wondering if she ought to ask to hop off. Take the ferry home.

"No, no, *no*." He shook his head then grabbed her hands. Clara startled, but Jake was calm. Even. "What happens if things *do* go well?"

～

THEY KISSED. They cuddled, and they kissed, and the boat rocked them like a lullaby until it was too cold to stay on the water any longer. And, until they'd drifted so far to the south side of the lake, they may as well reroute home.

"What are your plans for the rest of the night?" Jake asked as he slid back into his seat.

"Good question." Clara sighed contentedly and joined him at the center of the boat, two blankets wrapped around her. "Hot chocolate by the fire sounds perfect. Maybe a movie? And then essay grading, a little light reading, and early to bed."

"English teachers have as much homework as their students," he remarked.

Clara grinned. "More, I think. But I like it. I *love* it, in fact."

"It's important to have a passion in life. I try to tell Mercy that, but she doesn't understand."

Clara studied him thoughtfully for a beat. "What do you mean? Mercy seems like a passionate girl to me."

"She doesn't have a *thing*. You know? Me? I've got the lake—life in the lake and on the lake. Boats and..." He waved a hand to the shore. "...*broken buoy bells*." He chuckled. "I forgot that I was going to teach you about that."

"You still can. I love to learn. Just like your *daughter*."

He lifted an eyebrow to Clara.

"I think that's Mercy's passion in life. Learning."

Jake nodded slowly, and his grin turned to something else—something indefinable. "She likes reading, too, you know."

"I do know that." Clara had loaned Mercy dozens of books in their year and a half together.

"But it's not her main thing," Jake said, as though he was stuck in an internal conflict. "She doesn't have a *thing*. I worry about that. That she would be happy enough with her books and the internet and a local library—"

Clara laughed into the wind. "Jake, *listen* to yourself. Mercy's incredible for those very reasons. And more. She doesn't have to be a social whiz or a drama nerd. She can taste those things in moderate amounts, and that's okay, too."

"I'm that way, too, I guess. I like my down time."

"I guess all *three* of us are similar." Even as she said it, Clara wondered if it was a comment too far. A suggestion too intimate. Too presumptuous.

But Jake didn't seem to think so. "That's what I love about you, Clara."

Her face flushed, and her pulse throbbed. "You do?" She shook her head, flushing deeper. "I mean... it is?"

"Let's put it this way—if you were prowling parties and driving into the city every weekend to hit the nightclubs... well, let's just say I couldn't keep up."

Clara made a face. "Even in college, I wasn't much for parties."

"Me neither. Too focused on school."

"And you studied marine biology? Even in undergrad?"

"Undergrad was microbiology and marina industries—the second, I worked on during night classes at the community college. I just wanted to be on the water."

"And did you learn how to fix buoys back then?"

He chuckled as they approached the very one he'd mentioned had a problem. "I still don't know exactly how to fix buoys." He laughed to himself. "I had three different guys out here this past weekend. It took four of us to get everything back up to code, but we *still* had to call the Great Lakes Commission to guide us."

"Wow," Clara murmured as Jake slowed the boat not fifty yards off the shore of the Inn. "Did the previous marina manager sleep on the job or something?"

"I've been here for over two years. No reason I didn't catch the issues sooner. It's just that we're a bit of a sleepy hamlet in relation to other, bigger lakeside cities. I had never gone out at night before our date—at least, not in a little Bayliner."

She grinned to herself. By the time they docked, she and Jake would have been out three times on the water at or after dusk together.

Three times.

"All the buoys that belong to Birch Harbor were in disrepair? Lights out?" she asked, keeping the conversation going long enough to find a way to pivot into a dinner invitation. Or even just drinks. Dessert...

"Not all of them have lights, actually. Some are *only* bell buoys."

"They just needed... what? General maintenance?"

"Right, yeah. They hadn't been checked in a while. Well, the one by the church was fine. It's just a bell, you see. The ones near the harbor all have lights, and three of them had been updated more recently. One hadn't been checked in *years*, but it still works. Amazing, huh?"

"So, what about ours?"

"Yours?" Jake asked.

"Yes. I mean, I know the light was out. Had it been updated or anything?"

"Actually, no. It was in the worst shape. I would bet it has been *decades* since anyone touched that thing. We ended up putting in a request for a replacement, in fact. In the meantime, we added reflectors. See?" He pointed as they floated past.

"Oh, yes." But something caught her attention.

"You think the light was out for decades? Or just that it hadn't been *maintained* in decades?" Clara asked, her voice trembling, though not for the cold or the growing dark.

Jake heard it. Felt it. He must have. Because he killed the engine immediately and shifted in his seat. "I have no idea when the light was busted," he answered gravely. "But yes, Clara. It could have been out for many years. Especially if your family never noticed—"

"We didn't." Of this she was *positive*.

"You didn't what?" Jake asked slowly.

"We don't take boats out. We don't have guests boat in. Anyone who ever came to the house docked at the harbor. Mom refused to use our dock. It's old, and once Wendell left, she didn't keep it up. It's not safe. She didn't even like me swimming in the lake right off our shore."

"So, *nobody* docks at the Inn? Has Kate mentioned anything?"

Clara's mouth turned dry. A dull ache swelled in the hollow at the back of her neck. "No. No one docks at the Inn. Except..."

"Except whom?"

"Except Matt Fiorillo."

CHAPTER 53—KATE

Matt, Vivi, and Mercy had arrived first, before Kate even moved to call the others. Before Judith gave her that permission. Before she even asked.

Vivi's face was white and stricken. Mercy was dead quiet. Matt pushed a soggy-cornered file into Kate's hands and directed her out of the room, murmuring details about what the girls had found during their study session two nights earlier. What everyone else had *missed*.

It calmed Kate, in an odd way. As if all this time—ever since May... or earlier—she'd been waiting for something. Waiting for Nora to *really* die, perhaps. Waiting for someone else to die. Waiting for something—anything—to happen.

She didn't call her sisters then. She read the pages on her own. With no fanfare other than Matt's hands on her shoulders as she crumpled into a dining room chair.

The passages read clearly enough—Nora *had* gone to Gene.

She had interrogated him hotly, and she'd come up empty. But that wasn't all.

Another entry shed light on a different aspect of the ordeal.

A time that predated Wendell's disappearance. That predated even Clara...

But Kate didn't understand the entry's relevance.

Not immediately.

Matt had let her read it in silence, and then he'd held her before offering to make the calls. To gather the others. To meet with Judith and to put an *end* to the saga of Wendell Acton.

THEY SAT as a group in the parlor, and for whatever reason, it reminded Kate of the beginning.

Of Nora's funeral.

Instead of pretty, fragrant lavender plants, though, she had ferns and houseplants anchoring every table, every corner of the parlor. They'd soon be replaced with foil-sheathed pots of poinsettias and sprigs of holly and mistletoe.

Instead of distant relatives and cold strangers, it was those closest to Kate who sat in silence, waiting.

"Where *is* Clara?" Amelia asked for the umpteenth time. Kate watched as Michael moved a hand to her bouncing knee. He'd been first to storm in once Matt and the girls had settled there. Michael was excited to see Judith, apparently. Invested in the new information. As if something more depended on it. Something more than his passion for history or love of Birch Harbor.

Amelia was hot on his heels, asking why Judith couldn't just spit it out, but by then, Megan had called and declared that the girls had the missing pages—which, of course, they already knew. She'd passed the phone to Matt, who brought Megan up to speed in time for her and Sarah to barge through the doors themselves. Brian, too, was en route. It was important, Megan said. He ought to be there. Kate suspected this was Megan's way of having Brian present for a resolution, since he'd missed the *first* funeral.

"I told you, they're on the *lake*." Megan rolled her eyes and crossed her arms.

"Let's all just take a deep breath," Matt tried. Kate offered him a grateful look just as headlights flooded the room.

"It's them!" Mercy chirped from her station at the window.

"Don't bombard them," Kate warned, although no one budged. It was only Kate's energy, maybe, that couldn't be contained. Only Kate on the verge of hysteria. But it wasn't, of course. The others bubbled over, too.

When Kate opened the door, ready to brace Clara for what she was about to enter into, everything flipped on its head.

"Where is he?" she cried, her voice shaking. Jake stood behind her, nervous.

"Where is *who*?" Kate asked, bewildered.

"Matt. *Matt!*" Clara called past her.

Kate fell away from the door as Clara stormed in—out of character and out of her mind, maybe. "Matt," Clara's voice turned to a plea.

"Yes?" He was a deer in headlights, and all eyes settled on him. Like he had some answer. Like Clara had some question.

"The buoy bell." Clara threw a hand in the vague direction of the backyard. The lake. "The buoy bell behind our house."

Kate caught the slip—*our house*. Was it still that? Would the Inn ever be *just* the Inn? Kate hoped not. She couldn't help but let a smile creep up her face. How she wanted to reach out to Clara. To cradle her. To breathe the girl in like when Clara was first born.

"Sorry, Clara, I don't know what—"

"You come here all the time from the Island. You and Vivi." Clara's eyes flew to the girl. Was that what this was about? Had Clara found her voice? Was she disgruntled? Kate started to take a step to Matt but thought better of it and stayed put. Next to Clara.

"Right," Matt answered slowly, lowering himself onto the very edge of the sofa next to Vivi. Kate sensed sides were forming, and she didn't like it one bit.

"Have you ever been here at *night*, Matt?"

"*Clara*," Kate hissed, gripping her shoulder. She could feel Clara's collarbone—boney and sharp.

Clara rolled her shoulder back, shaking Kate's hand. "Mom—" Clara shook her head, blinked, and glanced at Kate. "I mean *Kate*."

But it was too late, and Kate's heart clung to that word. Congealed around it, taking it in and owning it as though she were a mother all over again. "What is this about, Clar?" Kate murmured softly.

"Jake *did* find something," Clara whispered back, loudly enough for all to hear, but her voice still rattled. "But we have to know. Matt—*please.*"

"Yes," he replied. "I've been here at night. Why?"

"Did you ever come here by boat at night when—when you were a kid? I mean when you all were kids?"

"What does this have to do with anything, Clara?"

Clara turned to Kate and grabbed her arm, pulling her

into the parlor and standing just in front of the window, her eyes wild. "The buoy bell that floats behind the Inn, the house, *whatever*—its light is out. And Jake thinks it hasn't been maintained in years. Maybe even decades." She turned to Matt, and her discomfort from before seemed to melt in front of Kate's eyes. "Matt, do you *ever* recall seeing the buoy bell lit up? How do you dock here? How did you dock here as a kid?"

He shook his head slowly. "That buoy never had a light. I'd remember. I mean... my boat has lights. I don't need the buoy to see, but we notice them when we're on the water. You know?" He searched the others for some form of valida-tion. Kate cocked her head toward him gently, mouthing that it was *okay*. It was *okay*. He went on, "And when we were kids, I drove here. Or walked, even. I didn't need a lit-up buoy for that."

"How did you get in the house back then?"

"What?" Matt asked, catching Kate's eye and frowning in confusion.

"When you snuck in, did you sneak in the front? The back?"

Matt chuckled nervously. "I didn't sneak in."

"Yes, you did." Kate propped her hands on her hips. "Of course you did. We were inseparable back then."

"Not much has changed," Vivi snorted. Kate lifted an eyebrow at her, and Vivi raised her hands. "Joking. I'm joking."

"No, it's true. I guess not much *has* changed."

"Everything has changed," Clara pointed out. "But that's not my question. So, there was *never* a working light on that buoy? You *swear*, Matt?"

He held up his hands. "As far back as I can remember, there was no light, Clara. I *swear*."

Clara grinned contentedly, but before she could go on, Kate waved her arms.

"Wait," she said. "The pages. The missing pages. That *entry*."

"Huh?" Clara shook her head.

Kate strode to the coffee table and collected them, flashing a quick look at Judith, who continued to sit motionless in the rocking chair.

"We found the missing pages. The girls did, rather. And Nora writes an entire entry about her regrets. She regretted making it easy for Matt and me to... well... *you* know."

"What?" Clara made a face.

"Here," Kate thrust the page at her. "Read it."

CHAPTER 54—NORA

WENDELL ACTON CASE

This entry has nothing to do with the case. It has only to do with what I did wrong. All the many things I did wrong.

I love my husband. I did that all too much. I loved Wendell so much that I trusted him. I trusted him when he locked the doors at night and tucked the girls into their beds.

I trusted him when the bills ran high and the money ran short.

I trusted him when he decided to stay in Birch Harbor and keep up appearances. I trusted him when he said he didn't mind if we left—he didn't mind if I took the girls and we left for a whole entire summer.

I trusted him when he agreed to play Clara off as ours. When he agreed that we'd brush it all under the rug.

I trusted him when he told me we could *talk* to Gene. That we could squash the rumors and keep her safe from the humiliation. That talking to Gene would solve everything.

I trusted Wendell, too, when he said Matthew Fiorillo was a good boy. A good boy who made a bad decision.

Mainly, though, what I did wrong was stop trusting Wendell as soon as I lost him.

But after I spoke with Gene, I realized that I could trust my husband again. That I could trust him all along.

That he was right *all along*. About everything.

And now I know that I didn't lose Wendell, in fact. Not in that way. And I now know that I'll see him again. One day, far off, when the girls are grown and happy. When they don't need me anymore.

I'll see him. And neither Wendell nor I will be lost.

And in the meantime, I have to trust that I can still live.

Even without him.

CHAPTER 55—CLARA

Clara looked up from the words. Her mother's words. Pained and choppy on the page. An accusation against herself. A lack of peace. And then, ultimately, a wobbly peace. The sort of peace you convince yourself to assume. Like a pep talk.

Clara's mind flew to the cross and the wreath. To the quiet nights and the loud ones. The dinner parties. The men who may have been dates—but who never did return.

All Clara's life, she had it wrong. She thought her mother had moved along at a nice clip—finding joy in filling her time with people and strangers, strangers and people. Society and attention and all the vapid things Clara had grown to loathe.

But Nora struggled all her life with moving on. A single tear budded along the edge of her eyelid, and Clara brushed it away. "Okay, so we know she talked to Gene. Maybe even *before* Wendell went... away?"

"I'm sorry, but I'm confused." Sarah raised her hand like she was in class.

"What is it, Sarah?" Clara pointed to her.

"What does the light have to do with anything?"

"It has to do with *everything*." Judith spoke, her tone a warning and an assurance all at once.

Everyone's eyes turned on the older woman, the Nora clone. The busy body. The middle-aged mean girl.

"Clara, Kate. Jake?" Judith said calmly. "You may want to sit."

CHAPTER 56—NORA

1993

"Gene? It's Nora. I need to talk to you." She shook in the chill of the night. Rain poured around the phone booth, and Nora felt ridiculous for calling from there. She could have waited until she got home. Clara cried in her car seat in the car. Lightning lit up the night sky.

"Nora? How are you?" his voice oozed like syrup—too sticky. Too sweet. It always had been.

"I can't talk long, but Gene, please. Have you seen him?"

"Seen who, Nora?"

"My *husband* Gene. Have you seen Wendell?"

"What are you *talking* about, Nora?"

"I asked have you *seen* Wendell Acton? Have you talked to him? Please Gene. I just—I have to know. I *have* to know."

Thunder cracked, and a baby's wail tore from the running car.

"Gene, I have to go. Please, just... can you answer my question, *dammit*?" She was a woman on the brink. On the verge.

"Nora, *calm down*. Where are you? Can I come meet you? Do you want to talk?"

"No, Gene, I want *you* to talk. *Now.* Or *else*, Gene."

"Or else *what*, Nora?"

"I'm working with Mathers. I meet him all the time. He's helping me, and he'll be interested to know about our history. I know he will."

"*Nora*," Gene hissed on the line. "Keep it *down.* Okay, listen, I *did* talk to him, but Mathers already knows this. I already came forward with it."

"Forward with *what*, Gene?"

"He wanted to talk about... about schooling options. About his concerns about the girls' schooling. I guess there had been an accusation of bullying, and he called me. We talked briefly. I assured him all was well. That was *it*, Nora. I promise."

"He doesn't know about us?"

"No, Nora. He doesn't know. The conversation *didn't* go there. I assure you."

CHAPTER 57—KATE

"Was that true?" Kate's lip quivered as she asked Judith. "Was it true that Gene didn't talk about the past with our father? Did Wendell find out? About Liesel? About Nora and Gene?"

Judith's eyes watered. "No. Gene told him."

A sob crawled up Kate's throat.

"No," Amelia cried. "It's *true*? Wendell found out about Nora and Gene, and... Wendell *left*." Her voice shook, and she rose from the sofa, but Michael pulled her down and rubbed her back.

Kate wiped her eyes with the backs of her hands.

"How did he react?" Megan managed through her own choked voice. Brian had arrived and sat on the floor beside her, holding her hands and shushing her softly.

"Wendell didn't go to Gene to talk about bullying. That was an untruth. He lied to Nora." Judith grimaced. "He lies often, I suppose, but I could tell he was being honest with me today. He had no choice, really."

"What do you mean?" Kate asked.

"I told him if he wasn't crystal clear and entirely honest, I was leaving him."

Kate frowned.

"I lied, too, I guess." Judith tried to suppress a grin, but it broke through. "I'm sorry. I know this is difficult to hear."

"Go ahead, Judith. Please," Michael asked.

"Gene told me that Wendell came to him ahead of Kate's return to school. You see, Wendell knew that—kids being kids—they had probably caught wind of the pregnancy. He worried about how her peers would treat her. How they'd *see* you when you came back, Kate."

Kate frowned. "I—it was fine." Her gaze flew to Matt before she looked at the others. "My sisters kept my secret well. My mother did, too. And if anyone knew—well, they said nothing. The year wasn't *normal*. I wasn't myself, but I never once heard someone whisper about me."

Amelia smirked. "If they *did* know, then they'd know that I'd have kicked their butts."

Kate smiled at her.

"Gene told me that he may have made a snide remark to your father about teen pregnancies running in the family." Judith worried her fingers together. "I'm so sorry he did that. He is too. Despite everything, I know he is."

"Wait," Kate held up her hand. "Gene suggested to Wendell that I came by teen pregnancy naturally or something?"

"Yes, and that's where *I* came into play."

The air hung heavily in the parlor. It was quiet enough to hear a pin drop.

Judith swallowed and shifted in the rocking chair. It creaked loudly, and she looked down. "I didn't know it then, I promise you. You see, from what I can gather, Wendell spoke to Gene about easing Kate back into school under her circumstances, and when Gene implied Nora had a history—Wendell put two and two together and made off for St. Mary's, where he, coincidentally, ran into me."

"And where you assured him that, what?" Amelia asked.

Judith's gaze fell as her chest rose. "I assured him that girls came to St. Mary's for any number of reasons—back in *those* days. But I also indicated, like I told you, that we didn't take young mothers particularly. Never had."

"And so he left thinking *what*?"

"He left, and it was late. It was *very* dark. I feel like the weather was bad, too. I—" she touched her fingers to her head and looked up. "Before he went, I told him something. This I *do* remember because he seemed so upset. So terribly upset, and I was a nun, of course, and so it was my duty to do *something*, you see."

"What?" Megan asked. "What did you *tell* him?"

"I said that whatever had happened to the girl in his life —and of course I was referring to what I thought must have been a daughter or maybe a young girlfriend of his—whatever had happened, it would be okay. I told him I would pray for him."

"And you didn't say this to the police?" Megan accused.

"I didn't *know*," Judith begged. "I was out of the loop. And by the time it all happened, my life was turning. Things were changing."

"So, he left?" Kate asked.

"Yes," Judith answered.

"And that's it?"

"Well, no. I mean—that's all I knew at the time. But today, when I spoke with Gene, I learned more."

"Go on," Michael urged her.

"Wendell called him, again, you see. After he left the

school, I suppose. Wendell demanded that Gene meet him at the house on the harbor."

"Why?" Kate asked. Matt squeezed her hand.

"Gene said that Wendell talked to a nun at the school and learned that Nora could have gone to St. Mary's for any reason under the sun. He didn't *believe* Gene. And he thought Gene was starting trouble, so he wanted to meet like men. Hash it out, I suppose."

Kate's breath hitched in her throat as she managed to review what Judith had just revealed. "He didn't think Mom had had a relationship with Gene?"

Judith smiled sadly. "No. He didn't believe it. And he wanted to take Gene to task for starting him off on such a tizzy, I suppose."

Amelia leaned forward, her cheeks ruddy and eyebrows low. "Then what happened?"

"Well, that's where the trail runs cold, I'm afraid," Judith confessed, holding her palms up. "Gene said he agreed to meet. He felt guilty about the whole thing and set off for the house on the harbor. He rang the doorbell for fifteen minutes, he says. No one ever answered. So, he left."

Quiet filled the parlor. A hardened silence.

"The bell," Clara whispered.

CHAPTER 58—MEGAN

They'd done it. They'd pieced it all together. With the help of Judith and Jake and Nora's notes, they'd established a firm theory on the case of the missing Wendell Acton.

But it wasn't until Jake established a diving team to search the lake bottom that the theory was confirmed.

And confirmed it was.

After two weeks of daily dives, they recovered more than he had expected. The boat had drifted in chunks all the way to the cove near the church. It was fate, Clara had said, that he'd wind up there, where Nora had left the wreath only the year before.

With the help of a friend of Michael's—a forensic specialist—they managed to recreate what might have happened. Wendell was worked up, emotional. His boat had no lights, and he relied only on those from the harbor. But according to Jake and Clara—who'd been on the water in that very spot—even with the harbor lights, it could be inky-dark and treacherous. Too dangerous, indeed. How Matt had managed to avoid a collision could only be explained by his familiarity with the buoy.

Wendell would have been familiar, too, but when they discovered evidence of both Wendell and his boat at the base of the buoy bell, the forensic specialist's speculation made sense. Wendell didn't see the buoy, hit it, struck his head somewhere in the boat, and fell overboard, drowning to his death. The boat would have sunk in a matter of hours to days, depending on the severity of the damage, the speed at which Wendell was going, among other factors. And since no one had searched for him immediately, it was reasonable to guess that the boat could have drifted relatively unnoticed the next morning—*if* it hadn't sunk overnight, which Michael's friend and even Jake believed it did.

The horror of it all had fallen like a shock on Megan and her sisters. For so long, they'd believed he'd left them. Purposefully, bitterly, and spitefully. And somehow, they accepted that. Needed that. Needed it to be an easy pill to swallow such as a deadbeat father story more often than not *was*. Nora had even *allowed* them to think he'd left.

Maybe that was the easy thing to do. Maybe it was easier than searching day in and day out as a troop of Hannigan women in a small town that had little interest. Maybe it was easier than what Nora hated to believe—that *she* had somehow caused it all.

By THE END of the two-week lake search, the coroner sent word that they could have a funeral.

A funeral, of all things.

Kate had suggested they wait—until warmer weather or a better time in their lives.

But Megan and Amelia had disagreed. Even Clara, who cherished the holiday season, had declared that she was *tired* of waiting.

So, that's what they did. They buried their father.

The service slid neatly between Christmas and Megan's *Twelve Dates of Christmas* event, and that was somehow— morbidly perhaps—perfect. It gave them closure. It gave them finality.

It gave them permission to finally and *truly* move on.

The funeral was an all-town affair. Nora would have been proud.

Reporters and distant relatives made their way down to the sleepy lakeside town, blanketed white by then. Local businesses offered to help with food and drinks for the service.

Megan joked that Wendell's funeral was a bigger event than any she would ever host in her life. Maybe it deserved a theme, like her other ones.

"It could have been *Death on the Dock*?" she said to Amelia after they'd left the cemetery, on their way back to the house on the harbor, where'd they'd reconvene for a private reception.

"No," Amelia replied. "Way too dark. Dad would have hated it. He was a classic sort of guy. You know?"

A distant moment tickled the back of her brain. The image of her father—kindly and rumpled, reading a newspaper in his easy chair, commenting mildly about the weather.

Amelia was right. He *was* classic. Classy, too.

"*Funeral on the Ferry*?" she tried, thinking more seriously about the idea. It was how she framed parts of her life now —naming them like episodes of a television show. Slotting them into position to log them away in her long-term memory.

"We didn't have his funeral on the ferry, though," Kate answered. She frowned. "Speaking of which, are you sure you still want to have your wedding there, Amelia? So soon after? And at the same place?"

A smile curled across Amelia's face, and she lifted her hand up, the antique gem sparkling anew after a recent cleaning and resizing. Amelia had changed in the short time since the discovery. Her skin was brighter. Her smile bigger. Her time with Michael more frequent, and her time with everything else less so. "That's the thing about life, Megan," Amelia said.

"What?" Megan asked.

"It's all a series of bells. Beginning with the striking of the clock at your birth, you're set off to a series of bells. School bells. Doorbells. Wedding bells. Buoy bells." Her voice dropped low. "The knell of the requiem bell, in the end." Then Amelia's face turned thoughtful. "Who knows? Maybe there's a bell in heaven, ushering in the new recruits, signaling soulmates back together after having been dearly departed."

Clara chimed in, "Bells, bells, bells."

And Kate added. "That can be your wedding, then, Am."

"What?" Amelia asked.

"Something *Bells*," Kate replied.

"*On the Bay*," Megan added, her eyes lighting up at the idea, happy to think ahead to the future—the bright, cheery future. The one they all deserved. They all longed for.

"I *love* it," Amelia whispered earnestly. "*Bells on the Bay*."

EPILOGUE

By May, things had changed dramatically in the lives of the four sisters, among other people of Birch Harbor.

Megan, Brian, and Sarah had moved into their new home in the field, and the trio was already planning a summer event for the ages: Sarah's graduation and farewell party.

Matt and Kate, with Vivi and Clara's blessing *and* presence, had eloped. They asked Sarah and Amelia to take over at the Inn for a week in March, and the four jetted away to Scottsdale, drinking in the warm spring days poolside after quiet vows in a pretty desert garden. Kate reported that it was nice to see Arizona in a different light, and even Clara felt a spark of some kind while there. The hint of a memory. Closure, too.

She still wouldn't call Matt her father after that trip. But she did call Vivi her sister.

Upon their return home, Jake had surprised Clara with his own romantic promise: he had purchased the property on Heirloom Island secretly. It was to be a place he'd like to share. Not only with Mercy, but with Clara, too. One day, maybe a couple of years from then, when Mercy was grown, and Clara was comfortable with the idea of becoming a stepmother.

Naturally, Mercy, Vivi, and Sarah discovered the secret land purchase and pieced together Jake's plan. But they did more with it, this time, than merely boating off into a treacherous cove with no plan to follow through. With Sarah's leadership, the girls rented the Birch Bell for a day and tricked Jake and Clara to board the ferry and sail over to the newly acquired property on the far side of the Island. There, the girls had set up a pretty picnic setting along an inland creek, much like the one at the back of the cottage.

And it was there that Jake, with Mercy's urging, proposed.

As for Amelia, well, her wedding didn't turn out quite as she'd originally planned.

With the closing of her father's case, she came to learn that all those years of running weren't in vain. The thing was Amelia wasn't running *from* something.

She was running *to* something.

To truth. To hope. And, to love.

Once she knew that, something in her changed. She wanted the biggest, craziest, happiest celebration on the lower peninsula. Or in all of Michigan. In all of the *world*.

Still, after the funeral and Megan's holiday mixer and Christmas, throwing a blowout wedding wasn't in the cards for Amelia and Michael. Not if they wanted to get married in early January.

Which they did. They *had* to, in fact.

So, the lovebirds ended up exchanging vows in an intimate Catholic Mass with just Amelia's sisters, their beaus, the girls, and Michael's cousin and his wife in January, as planned.

After, Amelia moved into Michael's house in Birch Harbor Heights. This allowed her to preserve the lighthouse as a true Birch Harbor museum *and* plan something far more extravagant for the ceremony. But come April, with Kate newly married and Clara newly engaged, the idea of *Bells on the Bay* had taken on a whole new shape.

With Amelia and Michael's hearty support, Megan spun the event into a family-wide celebration of love—a May event where they'd not only enjoy the quaint, meaningful venue that was the Family Hall, but also the sandy space of Birch Bay.

Invitations included all the major players in town: Mayor Van Holt, the Fiorillo family, half of the faculty at Birch Harbor High and even some of the ones from the junior high. Jake's deckhands. The Birch Players. Michael's secretary. Paige and her family.

And, naturally, Judith Carmichael.

Or, rather, Judith *Banks*.

After the dust had settled on Wendell, Judith secured a quick divorce with Gene. Michael, who'd formerly represented Gene, couldn't act in offense or defense for the Carmichael case. He excused himself from any involvement. However, he had a good friend in the business who was happy to come back and help: Zack Durbin, who had maintained his Michigan practicing license over the years. With Zack's help, Judith washed her hands of the smarmy boathouse dweller *and* erected a civil suit on behalf of the Hannigan-Acton family for damages.

They won, and earnings were split *equally* among the four sisters to do with as they pleased.

The timing of the lawsuit and the divorce made it easy

for Judith to maintain their house in Harbor Hills, while Gene was forced to sell his houseboat and disappear forever. Unfortunately for him, there were no daughters to take up the search once he was gone.

As *Bells on the Bay* roared into the night, the sisters tucked themselves away on the dock. Just the four of them together, before the night drifted away—before Sarah and the girls got silly and tired. Before Amelia, now six months pregnant and *always* tired, needed to go rest. Before anyone else could elbow her way into their tight clique.

"What time did she say she'd be here?" Megan asked Kate, squinting through the lamplit grass to the parking lot beyond.

"I mean, she should have been here first thing. Matt gave her the right time."

"Ladies!" a voice called out at the edge of the dock.

The women turned. It was Father Vann and with him, Michael, who held a life buoy.

Amelia's eyes narrowed on it as the two men approached. "Is that—?" she asked, pointing.

Michael nodded. "You were right. Look."

Father Vann shone his flashlight on the back of the white ring and there, plain as day, was scrawled in faded black marker *Birch Harbor Lighthouse.*

Amelia had told Michael about her hunch regarding the piece of décor in the church offices, but it wasn't until tonight that he'd remembered to look.

Sad smiles spread across the faces of the women. "I think we know where that belongs," Amelia replied.

The others murmured their agreement, and Michael leaned in to kiss his wife, his hand resting on her growing bump.

Amelia knew better than to stand for long. Her age

added complications to her condition, but she was doing well enough as long as she took it easy. The women considered Amelia's baby to be a miracle child, and they treated her as a special case. She didn't mind the attention.

"Let's head back," Amelia said to the others.

Kate hooked an arm underneath Amelia's, and the group moved to a set of wooden Adirondack chairs, the ones Matt had hauled over from the house on the harbor.

As Amelia lowered herself into one, Judith appeared. "Amelia, how are you doing, dear?"

"Oh, fine. Really fine, actually. Just tired."

The other three sisters settled into their own chairs, and Judith perched on the bench nearest Amelia. She'd become close to them. Not a mother figure. No way. But something like that. Protective.

And the sisters were protective of Judith, too. She'd lived in the Inn with Kate during the divorce, cleaning and helping a great deal—and inspiring Kate to officially hire live-in help. This also allowed Kate to move in with Matt once she could entrust the house on the harbor with a few capable innkeepers.

"Amelia," Clara prodded, "You haven't told Judith the name yet."

Judith's face lit up. "Oh, you've picked a name? Then you know the gender, too?"

"Yes," Amelia answered, regaining her energy at the question. "We found out a little later. I wasn't sure I wanted to know, you know?"

"It's a boy," Kate blurted out, but Amelia just laughed lightly. Her sisters would be as much a mother to the precious little life as Amelia was, at least, if *she* had any say.

"Wendell Hannigan Matuszewski," she beamed.

Judith's face crumpled, and she gushed, "It's *perfect*. A little bit of everyone."

"I think you should call him Dell," Megan said.

"I like that." Amelia smiled.

Clara shifted forward in her seat, her expression tightening as she pointed a discreet finger behind them. "Is that *her*?" she asked the others.

All five pairs of eyes laser-focused on a female shape in the grass.

She stood with Matt, and although a veritable stranger to the Hannigans, she was all-too familiar.

"What's her name again?" Megan asked, her voice ice.

"Quinn," Kate replied mildly.

"And why is she here again?" Megan went on.

"It was my idea," Kate answered. "I told Matt it wasn't healthy. He can't continue to give in when Vivi refuses to visit her."

"Why does Vivi refuse?" Amelia asked. "There must be a reason."

Clara responded, "She doesn't like Detroit, mainly."

"That's it? That's why she doesn't want to be with her own mother?" Megan scoffed.

"Who knows the full story?" Kate said. "Ever since I moved in, I realized that there was a bigger picture. Honestly, it seems like a case of an aloof father." Kate winced. "But that's why Matt needs me. To help bridge the divide. A woman's touch."

"How can they bridge the divide if the woman lives in Detroit?" Megan asked.

"Actually," Kate answered, "She's house-hunting this weekend."

Clara gasped. "Here? In Birch Harbor?"

Kate shrugged. "Wherever she can find a place that's closer."

"What about The Bungalows?" Amelia suggested.

Kate shook her head. "Too close for comfort."

Judith piped up. "I know of a place that just hit the market."

The others broke their gaze from the white-blonde woman in the grass and turned to Judith.

"You do?" Kate asked.

"On my street. It's a foreclosure."

"In Harbor Hills?" Clara asked.

"Yes. It's on Apple Hill Lane. It's a project, but it might be perfect."

Thank you so much for reading Birch Harbor. If you join my newsletter, you'll be the first to know when I release new books. Visit elizabethbromke.com to learn more.

What's more, Birch Harbor may be over, but Harbor Hills has only just begun. Start the new series by ordering The House on Apple Hill Lane *today.*

ALSO BY ELIZABETH BROMKE

Birch Harbor:

House on the Harbor

Lighthouse on the Lake

Fireflies in the Field

Cottage by the Creek

Bells on the Bay

Harbor Hills:

The House on Apple Hill Lane

Gull's Landing:

The Summer Society

The Garden Guild

The Country Club

Hickory Grove:

The Schoolhouse

The Christmas House

The Farmhouse

The Innkeeper's House

The Quilting House

ACKNOWLEDGMENTS

Writing Birch Harbor has been a joy and a pleasure in *great* part thanks to a few key players.

Elise Griffin, thank you for being such an important partner in my writing. You make me better with each chapter!

Sue Soares and Krissy Moran, thank you for your careful eyes and kindhearted support.

Wilette Cruz, this series began with *you*. Your beautiful covers inspired my stories and pulled people into the little lakeside town. Thank you for being a critical part of my career.

My dear advanced readers: thank you for being my unsung heroes. You cheerlead for me and help me through the hardest part of publishing a book: those first sets of eyes... the early reviews... the nerve-racking days when I question everything!

I have been lucky to gain several "writing sisters" over the past couple of years. Without them, this journey would be a lonely one. A few include Mel, Rachael, and Gigi.

Ladies, thank you for being a part of my everyday life—for your honesty and friendship.

I'm very fortunate to have a family who believes in me and supports my creative efforts. Ed, thank you for ALL that you do for us. I love you!

Eddie—always you! Always!

ABOUT THE AUTHOR

Elizabeth Bromke writes women's fiction and contemporary romance. She lives in the northern mountains of Arizona with her husband, son, and their sweet dog, Winnie.

Learn more about the author by visiting her website at elizabethbromke.com.